DOROTHY CLAES

AND THE

PRISON OF THENEMI

DOROTHY CLAES

AND THE

PRISON OF THENEMI

THE SILVER FOX MYSTERIES

BOOK ONE

C.P. MORGAN

Ordering Information:
www.authorcassandramorgan.com
www.amazon.com

First Printing: March 2018
White Whisker Publications

ISBN: 978-1-7321398-2-4

This book is for my grandmothers,
Shirley and Jackie.

And for all the ladies who have earned their wisdom
highlights: never forget you're still a badass.

Special thanks to:
Sandra Hults, Catherine, Amber, Robin Austin,
Theresa Jacobs, and Kris McClain.

❀NE

THE LITTLE BRASS KEY IN DOROTHY'S HAND was like ice against her bones. She closed her palm and opened it again, reciting the words from her father's will over and over in her mind.

> *I devise, bequeath, and give my antique store, Richard's Anecdotes, to my daughter, Dorothy Virginia Shirley Claes, in the hopes she can find roots while surrounded by the lore of the world she loves so dearly.*

A bitterly cold January wind beat hard against the side of her face. Finally, she gave in and unlocked the door to Richard's Anecdotes.

The security alarm beeped wildly, and she hurried to punch in the code the estate attorney had given her. Despite the fact no one had set foot in her father's little shop for at least a week, it was practically spotless. She wiped a finger across a silver platter, and only the faintest bit of dust could be seen. Richard Van Damme had kept a tight ship and a tidy store. But Dorothy would leave that task to her father's – now her – assistant for later.

She glanced around the little antique shop once more before setting a cat carrier on the floor at her feet. She opened the door, and a small black cat leapt out. It immediately began winding itself around the woman's legs, purring loudly. She was careful not to step on the cat's paws or tail as she picked her way past the neatly organized tables and bureaus to the back of the shop. There, a door leading up to the second-story apartment stood facing her. It was painted a bright, sickly avocado green. She had always hated that color. It would be the first thing to change.

The apartment had been her father's office and storage area, where antiques were kept until they could be appraised or even repaired. But the estate sale had cleared out almost everything, save for the old mahogany desk and a few odds and ends. The movers would arrive tomorrow with the rest of Dorothy's things. The woman sighed, still staring at the avocado green door. She reached for the handle. She might as well get any uncomfortable emotions out now. It would be an awful embarrassment to everyone if she started blubbering about her father as her couch was being carried up the stairs.

The cat bounded up the floral carpeted steps ahead of her and disappeared around the corner toward the little sitting area and kitchenette. Dorothy followed and plunked herself at her father's desk, which sat perched on the wide landing at the top of the stairs. She ran her hands over the worn leather of the chair arms and stared at the last notes he had scribbled before passing in his sleep. There was the typical appraisal information for new pieces he had collected. Against Dorothy's better judgment, her sister, Mary Pat, had insisted on letting them go in the estate sale. A three-month-old electric bill and a phone number for a Destin Hollanday lay across the keyboard.

Dorothy didn't touch them. She wasn't ready to disturb them quite yet. Mary Pat, on the other hand, had dived headfirst into organizing and dealing out their father's possessions. Dorothy supposed everyone had their own methods for coping. She sat in silence for several long minutes, watching Solomon run back and forth through the apartment. He was far more excited to be here than she was. She opened the top drawer of the desk and found a sticky note wrapped around an antique skeleton key.

"For Dorothy," it read. "The Silver Fox."

The cat jumped on the desk with a purring trill and rubbed its head against Dorothy's hands.

"Not now, Solomon," she whispered to the cat.

Solomon licked his paw twice before tearing off with another buzz after Lord knew what. Dorothy had adopted the cat while visiting the temples in Taiwan five years ago. She had known then the cat was going to be a handful as a kitten, but his energy hadn't seemed to lessen. She wasn't disappointed, however. Solomon had become her constant companion since her husband, Frank, had passed away three years ago. That cat had probably seen more of the world in a single year than most humans would see in a lifetime.

Dorothy had retired as the curator to the Boston Museum of Fine Arts when she'd turned fifty-six. There had been a lovely going-away party, complete with gifts, balloons and a giant cake frosted to look like Monet's *Water Lilies*. That had been nine years ago. She and Frank had decided to sell nearly everything they had and travel the world. They'd never stayed in one place for more than a few months before finding somewhere new to fly off to. It had been a dream that Dorothy would never have experienced without her husband's adventurous spirit.

Five years into their whirlwind travels, Frank was

diagnosed with stage 4 lung cancer. They immediately returned to the US for treatment, but it was to no avail. Frank's passing had been the hardest thing Dorothy had ever had to endure. Death was the greatest mystery of the world, dating back to the beginning of time. It was her only true fear, and she had not been prepared for it when it had come for Frank.

Dorothy found herself pacing through the upstairs apartment, the key and sticky note held tight to her chest. She shook her head and headed for the little kitchenette. She set a kettle to boil some water for tea and flopped into one of the only remaining chairs left in the apartment. She watched as Solomon jumped on the bookcase and sent a cascade of books to the floor.

"Dang it, cat!" she cried. She rose and heard her left knee give a resounding crack. The cold had never been kind to her, especially after she had decided to train and compete in a national jiu-jitsu competition in her forties.

Dorothy bent to pick up a handful of the antique books when she noticed a single tome that had remained upright despite its neighbors' plummet to the floor. *The Silver Fox.* Dorothy looked at Solomon, who sat on the chair grooming his tail. She stared at the key still clenched in her hand.

"This is ridiculous," she whispered to herself. She

shoved the key into her pocket and resumed picking up the books.

Solomon looked up from his bath and sat alert, his bright green eyes alight with the mischief and wonder only a cat could understand. He meowed once at her, turned a circle in the chair and sat back down again.

Dorothy set the books back on the shelf. She stared at The Silver Fox book and heard Solomon meow behind her again.

"I guess it wouldn't hurt," she said, more to herself than the cat, and reached for the book. It was stuck firmly to the shelf. She worried something had spilled and cemented the book in place. She pulled again, and this time it broke free and fell toward her as though on a hinge. A lever popped out from the side of the shelf. The sense of wonder Dorothy felt each time she visited someplace new filled her. Her bones no longer ached from the wretched weather. Her hearing and vision seemed to have sharpened. She pulled the little lever and the bookcase swung toward her.

Solomon immediately jumped from the chair and darted through the narrow passageway. The stairs were steep and the cat disappeared within moments.

"Solomon!" Dorothy called and scrambled for her cell phone. She switched on the flashlight and headed down the stone steps.

The stairs wound in a tight spiral, and the brick looked original to the building – late 18th century. Dorothy had found evidence of other secret passages in Lexington, Massachusetts, so its existence was not a surprise. What was surprising was why her father had never mentioned it before.

The steps twisted farther than the main level. There was no basement to her father's shop that Dorothy knew of. The steps ended at a short hallway and a large metal door that loomed ominously at the far end. Solomon sat outside the door as though waiting for her. He gave a sort of purring-buzz when he saw her and walked in a circle excitedly.

Dorothy lifted the skeleton key to the lock, her hands trembling. The tumbler rotated with a loud clang that echoed in the tiny space. She scooped Solomon into her arms and pushed the door open.

It was pitch black, save for what Dorothy's phone flashlight roamed over. Tables and shelves stretched far longer than the little shop above and were filled with objects much older than anything in her father's store. There were ancient scrolls stored beneath glass and strange pieces of jewelry, trinkets and other oddities that lined the shelves. The skeleton of a giant winged creature hung from the ceiling. It nearly gave Dorothy a heart attack when her light flashed over it.

An antique telephone rang somewhere to her left. Solomon fluffed and leapt from her arms, and Dorothy fumbled with her cell phone. She lifted the receiver from the base and held it up to her ear.

"H-Hello?" she said, trying to keep her voice from shaking.

"Ms. Claes," said a man's voice.

"Y-Yes," said Dorothy.

"Would you be so kind as to turn on the lights? You'll find a lever beside the door you entered. The lights need some time to warm up before they are fully functional."

Dorothy shined her cell phone light back toward the door and saw a large lever embedded in the wall. She set the receiver on the table and walked to the lever. Solomon beat her to it. She pulled hard, and immediately lights flickered to life throughout the room. She stared in wonder at the sights that met her eyes.

She ran back to the antique phone. "What is going on?"

"Yes, I understand it is rather much to take in unexpectedly. I would be more than happy to discuss this with you further. I am waiting at your front door. May I come in?"

"How did you know I was down here?" she asked.

"If you will look at the door again, you will see a small sensor at the top of the door frame. Richard had it installed about a year ago when he first discovered his illness."

"What illness? My father wasn't ill! The doctors said he passed of age."

"Ms. Claes, I am afraid there are many things about Richard Van Damme that you do not know. But they are all things he wished to pass on to you. Now, it is very cold out here, madam. I would love nothing more than to discuss this further with you over a cup of tea."

"Who are you?" Dorothy asked in an awed whisper.

"My name is Destin. Destin Hollanday. I work as a consultant, mostly to the Worchester Museum of Art. You are more than welcome to look up my credentials, but I would beg you to do so after you have let me in out of the cold."

Dorothy slammed the phone down and bolted up the winding stairs. She was thankful she had maintained a very active lifestyle, even into her elder years. Her knees creaked at the effort, but she was barely out of breath when she reached the top of the stairs. Solomon bounded through the bookcase and Dorothy pushed it shut. She ran back to her father's desk and pulled a tiny Smith & Wesson she carried with her from her purse. She locked Solomon in the bathroom to keep him out of the way before heading down the apartment stairs.

A gentleman in his late fifties stood outside the front door of the little shop. He wore a woolen trench coat and a black homburg. He smiled and waved when he saw her. Dorothy clutched the pistol even tighter in her pocket. She unlocked the door and Destin Hollanday pushed it open.

"Thank you, dear lady," he said.

The tea kettle began to whistle upstairs and Destin smiled. "What wonderful timing," he said, heading for the avocado green door. His hand had barely rested on the knob when he stopped. Dorothy held her gun between his shoulder blades.

"I don't know what's going on here, but you're going to tell me everything right now," she seethed.

Destin sighed. His hands slowly moved above his head in surrender. Without warning, he spun around faster than Dorothy would have expected of a man his age. He twisted the gun from her grasp and immediately emptied the chamber into his palm before tossing the gun back to her.

"My dear woman, I promise you have no idea what you are dealing with."

TWO

THE DAMN CAT IS A TRAITOR, DOROTHY thought as she watched Solomon wind himself around Destin Hollanday's ankles, purring like an innocent kitten. Dorothy glared at the scene from where she sat in the old armchair. Destin had pulled around her father's office chair from the study opposite them and proceeded to make himself at home, blowing across the top of the cup of hot tea. He had removed his coat and hat and had made himself quite comfortable in the tiny apartment. He set the little cup on the bookcase beside him and smoothed his graying hair.

"First, let me say, I'm sorry about your father," Destin began. Dorothy bit her cheek and looked away. "He was a good friend. He will be missed by everyone, not just the foxes."

The old woman's eyes narrowed as she turned back

to the strange man. "I can't imagine how difficult it must be to lose someone you barely knew," she snapped.

The man leaned forward in his chair. "I can say with certainty there were things about Feli – Richard that I did not know. But, the same can be said for you, madam."

"If you are implying my father's illness –"

"I am implying much more than that." Destin reached into his jacket pocket. Dorothy could hear the clinking of the bullets as he did so. She clutched at the small gun she still held in her hand. But the man extracted a folded picture and handed it to Dorothy.

Her father stood in front of an old airplane surrounded by at least a dozen other people. Men, women, and all seeming to represent different parts of the world. A plump Indian woman in bright clothing stood to Richard's left. A man with a head of bright white hair stood behind him, giving Richard little bunny ears. You could almost hear him laughing. Chinese, African, American, they were all there, smiling with Richard at their center. Dorothy had never seen any of these people in her life. Her heart dropped when she realized Destin Hollanday may have been correct after all.

"This was taken the day your father retired from

field work," said Destin. "We set up a case for him, even had Artie pick him up. We flew him all the way to Abu Dhabi. He loved the cuisine there. When he exited the plane, they were all there, waiting for him. I took the picture."

"Who are they?" Dorothy asked. Her voice was much calmer than she felt. Solomon left his spot beside Destin's ankles and climbed onto her lap. He rubbed his face under her chin, and she nonchalantly scratched the nape of his neck, not daring to take her eyes off the picture.

"The Silver Foxes. They were your father's friends and colleagues. Men and women from across the world who work for a small branch of the UN. There are things in this world that all nations can agree we need to protect ourselves from."

"And my father worked as a field agent for this UN department?" She raised an eyebrow at Destin. Solomon meowed. Dorothy wasn't sure if he was agreeing with her question, or whether he wanted his afternoon treat.

Destin nodded. "You see, our foxes are ordinary people in their countries. They can take the tube to the grocery store without a second look. They understand the art of casual small talk and how to appear just a step less than perfect at all times. These people are not only masters of their trades – and often chosen for those careers – they are masters of blending in. Heads might turn at the lovely blonde-haired beauty who could pass for a Hollywood actress, even after a kickboxing session. But our foxes," a smile curled Destin's lips and he nodded his head, "our silver foxes are conveniently glanced over."

Dorothy leaned back in her armchair. Solomon took the opportunity to use her shoulder as a launch pad to jump over the back of the chair and race down the apartment stairs.

"And what exactly do these silver foxes do for the UN?" she asked.

Destin took a slurping sip of his tea and stood.

"Let me show you." He reached toward the bookcase and pulled the book that opened the secret passage.

Solomon bolted back up the stairs from the shop and stood in the bookcase's frame. He sniffed the air before taking off down the dark and winding steps.

Dorothy looked from the passageway to Destin, her hands clutching at the arms of her chair.

Destin reached into his pocket and removed one of the bullets. He handed it to Dorothy and headed down the stairs after Solomon. She could hear his footsteps moving farther down the stone steps. When she could no longer hear his footfalls, she loaded her Smith &

Wesson and followed.

Destin stood waiting at the end of the long hall. He turned the handle to the heavy door and held it open for her. Solomon bounded in, and Dorothy hurried after him.

The light that fell across the giant skeleton made the creature look even larger, though Dorothy's heart now pounded for different reasons.

Destin approached one of tables and unlatched a glass box. He lifted a pair of diamond earrings with his handkerchief.

"The jewels of Marie Antoinette were renowned," he said. Dorothy stepped closer, her eyes flicking from Destin to the shining diamonds. "She lost most of her jewels during the French Revolution. These examples of wealth became a symbol of hatred for the French populace. In time, they came to resent anything that represented the lavish lifestyle of the monarchs and political heads."

Gently, Destin set the diamond earrings back into their glass box and closed the lid.

"Your father found these back in the 80's. A recently wealthy French family had found themselves the victims of what they called a curse. Little white lies grew bigger and bigger, and anyone who wore these earrings succumbed to an untimely death."

Destin moved down the line to the next glass box. This one, he did not open. He ran his finger across the surface of the glass, and the contents within flashed green.

Solomon jumped on the table and pawed at the glass box. Dorothy quickly scooped him up, brushing cobwebs from his face and ears.

"Have you ever seen the sun set over the ocean, Dorothy?" he asked.

Dorothy swallowed and replied, "yes."

"And have you seen the fabled green flash just before the sun sinks below the horizon?"

"Yes."

Destin turned back to the box. "Lesser men than our late agent, Jorge, have fallen victim to a siren's call. I don't recommend you open this one."

He turned toward the room, throwing his arms wide. "Each of these artifacts has a power the world does not understand. If they were to ever find them…" Destin turned to face Dorothy, his lips still curled in a curious smile. "I devise, bequeath, and give my antique store, Richard's Anecdotes, to my daughter, Dorothy Virginia Shirley Claes, in the hopes she can find roots while surrounded by the lore of the world she loves so dearly," Destin repeated the words from Richard's will. Dorothy felt numb. She let the words wash over her, suddenly finding new meaning in them.

"Hello? Ms. Class?" called a voice from above them.

"Ah, it's Aaron," Destin said quietly.

Dorothy adjusted Solomon in her arms and headed for the door. Her father's assistant must have arrived for his late morning shift. Dorothy hadn't realized what time it was. She hurried up the stone steps, Solomon wiggling in her grasp. For a moment, she considered locking Destin in the passage. His talk of magical artifacts had her head spinning, and she had more questions than answers.

"Ms. Class?" said Aaron's voice again, much closer to the avocado green door this time.

"I'll be there in a moment!" she called, closing the bookcase behind Destin and watching as Solomon zoomed down the apartment stairs to the newcomer. Her head snapped back as Destin picked up his coat from Richard's desk. He reached into his pocket and set the remaining bullets on top of the sticky note with his name and phone number.

"Keep the picture," he said. He situated his hat over his silver hair and headed for the stairs. Dorothy followed close behind.

"Oh, Mr. Hollanday," Aaron said. He set Solomon on the floor and reached out a hand toward the man.

"I didn't realize you were here."

"No worries, my boy." Destin shook Aaron's hand and reached down to offer Solomon a last pet and ear scratch. "Your semester finals are coming up?"

Aaron shook his head, his tightly coiled dreadlocks swaying behind him. "No, sir. Last week. The art department gets out a week earlier for Christmas break. But then we start a week earlier."

Destin nodded and clapped Aaron on the shoulder. "You keep it up, young man. Ms. Claes here is much stricter than Mr. Richard. Your grades will matter to this one." He smiled at Dorothy over his shoulder and headed for the door. Dorothy stood still, watching him leave until he had turned out of sight from the side window.

"Uh, Ms. Claes?" Aaron said tentatively. Dorothy turned her attention back to the young man before her.

"Aaron, I'm sorry," she apologized and stepped off the last stair. She transferred the gun to the hand holding the picture and reached to shake his. "It's a pleasure meeting you again. And, yes, it's Claes. Like Case, but with an L."

"Yes. I'm sorry. And, I am sorry about your father. I appreciate you keeping me on."

Dorothy smiled. "An art student after my own heart? And my father loved you, Aaron. I wouldn't dream of letting you go."

Aaron shifted sheepishly, his teeth flashing a bright smile against his ebony skin.

"Do you need this cataloged?" he asked and pointed to the Smith & Wesson in Dorothy's hand.

"Oh, no. This is mine. I was showing it to Mr. Hollanday." Dorothy shot a look at the front door.

"Ah." Aaron nodded, then bent to pet Solomon. "Do you want me to start moving the cases back? I know your family needed them moved to clear out Richard's apartment."

Dorothy looked around at the antiques that had been haphazardly stacked and the heavy cases that had been pushed to the side to make room for the furniture and boxes from the upstairs apartment.

"No. The movers will be delivering my things tomorrow. There's no point in us doing twice as much work."

Aaron nodded again. "Should I keep researching the Auritean texts, then?"

"The what?"

Aaron walked to one of the cases that had been moved. He slid aside the back panel and grabbed a pair of white gloves. He put them on and carefully pulled out a scroll like the one Dorothy had seen earlier in the strange basement room.

"I'm not a linguist, so it's taking me some time, but I think I have identified the parchment material."

"This looks like Sanskrit." Dorothy eyed the parchment with the same scrutiny she had used when she'd been a curator. She had a knack for finding fakes and seeing things where others didn't.

"Richard said the same thing," said Aaron, "but there are enough differences to dismiss it. There's even a few Grecian influences." He unraveled the parchment a bit more. "If I didn't know better, I'd say this was written by someone who was bilingual, but they got some of the translations incorrect and filled in with their native language."

"This looks like Futhark," Dorothy whispered as she pointed to a strange, triangular symbol at the end of one of the lines.

"Not Futhark. The pattern of strokes indicates that's a dot in the center, not a line."

Dorothy stood straight again. "What was my father having you research this for? Do we have a buyer?"

Aaron shrugged. "I'm not sure, ma'am. He brought it back from one of his travels and asked me to identify it. Wouldn't say no more."

"What sort of travels did my father go on?" Dorothy squinted at the boy and Aaron took a step back.

"I supposed they were business trips to get new

antiques. He often called and asked me to research things for him while he was away."

Solomon pawed at Dorothy's pant leg and meowed pitifully. She looked at the grandfather clock by the door and saw it was nearly noon.

"For now, try to clean where you can. It will be less work when we need to put things back together tomorrow. After that, you go and enjoy your time off class. I can handle things here for a few days. I'll see you on Monday, Aaron." She smiled and patted the boy's arm.

Solomon darted ahead of her toward the stairs, trilling and meowing. Dorothy followed in a daze. She pulled the cat's treats out of her purse and fed him without even counting out the pieces.

Destin's cup of tea sat innocently on the bookcase. She sat in the armchair and smoothed the picture across her lap. Her father's face smiled up at her, and her stomach dropped. She felt hot tears sting her eyes. This time, she did not hold them back. Solomon jumped onto her lap, sending the picture to the floor. He rubbed his whiskers and nose across her cheeks, wiping away the tears and wetting his black fur. He settled onto her lap and placed his chin on her chest. Dorothy wrapped her arms around the cat and sobbed.

THREE

A GENTLE SNOW HAD BLANKETED THE LITTLE Massachusetts town that night. Dorothy's bones ached from the biting cold. She much preferred the South Carolina climate she had lived in before her father had passed. She rubbed some warming cream into her joints and donned her purple reflective tracksuit.

Solomon stretched and yawned at the end of the air mattress. He blinked, then seemed to think better of the idea of getting up so early. He flopped back on his side and placed a paw over his eyes. Dorothy smirked at him, scratched behind his ears, and headed down the stairs to the antique store.

It was still dark, but the street lights that reflected off the snow illuminated the street in a soft, yellow glow. Dorothy scooped out a cupful of salt from the bin by the front door and sprinkled it in front of the store. She tossed the cup back into the container and locked the door behind her.

Her shoes crunched on the thin layer of snow as she began a slow and easy jog. She breathed steadily, her breath coming in thick, white clouds that quickly dissipated. In a roundabout way, her father had been the one to inspire her morning jogs.

After a break-in at the museum, Dorothy had felt compelled to learn how to defend herself, and Richard had been the one to suggest jiu-jitsu. Dorothy had managed to work her way into the women's national competition, even though she was already in her early forties at the time. Jogging had helped her learn to steady her breathing and heart rate under pressure. She no longer practiced jiu-jitsu but continued to jog every morning.

A few shopkeepers had arrived early to shovel the bit of snow from outside their stores. Dorothy stopped on a street corner, jogging in place until a salt truck had passed by. She rounded the corner, heading back toward the shop. She could now see the faintest glow of orange through the trees that lined the street.

She looked at her watch and started running faster. Her mind began to race in time with her footfalls. Dorothy had sent the ominous scroll Aaron had shown her to a friend at the Smithsonian yesterday.

There was something strange about it, and something just as strange about that Destin Hollanday fellow. The picture he had given her flashed in her mind's eye, and she stumbled a bit on the thin layer of snow.

Her family had never been one for practical jokes, save for her nephew, but even this was beyond Craig to dream up. That picture did not look fabricated. And the way Mr. Hollanday had so easily disarmed her indicated he was someone who had experience and muscle memory with such things. It was unnerving. Dorothy felt a shiver run down her spine, and it was not the cold.

What was more, the idea that magical artifacts existed throughout the world was baffling. Marie Antoinette's earrings had been endowed with power from the hatred of the French revolutionists? At least that was slightly easier to imagine than the belief that sirens existed.

She slowed her pace a block from the shop and walked the rest of the way. She was surprised to find the moving truck already parked outside the store. She fumbled for the key to the door but noticed the truck cab was empty.

She could hear Solomon scratching at the door to the stairs when she entered. She opened the avocado green door and almost tripped on Solomon as he wound himself excitedly about her ankles. She climbed the stairs and tossed her gloves and coat on her father's desk. Solomon ran past in a blur of black fur and eager meowing.

"I'm coming," she said as he jumped onto the small stove. She pulled a can of cat food from a grocery bag and set it on the floor in the bathroom. The cat's food dishes were on the moving truck, but he didn't seem to mind eating out of the tin. She tossed a few toys into the bathroom before shutting him in with his food. He had yet to figure out how to open this particular door, and Dorothy hoped the food and toys were enough to distract him before he did so. The last thing she needed was for him to bolt while the movers had the front door propped open.

She peeked out the second-story window. There was still no one in the truck. It was barely 7:00, and they weren't scheduled to arrive until eight. She hoped they had only slipped off to the coffee shop a few blocks away, but she couldn't help but be concerned that something else was going on. Her encounter with Destin Hollanday had her seeing conspiracies everywhere.

She stripped off her jogging clothes and hurried through the shower. Of course, Solomon had finished his food by the time she stepped out, and she had to appease him with jingle balls and catnip.

At 8:00 sharp, she saw three men walking up the street, cups of steaming coffee in hand. They all wore the same jacket with the moving company's logo on the front. Dorothy caught herself sighing aloud.

She hurried down the apartment stairs and unlocked the front door.

"Good morning, gentlemen," she said with a smile. The men smiled back at her, though their expressions seemed as frozen as their fingers. They shivered against the cold as they nodded in turn, giving a curt "ma'am" as they did so.

"Please, come in. I'll show you to the apartment." She held the door open for them, and they followed Dorothy up the narrow stairs.

After several minutes of taking measurements, moving more display cabinets and laughing at Solomon's paw swipes from under the door, the three movers began the tedious work of unloading Dorothy's possessions. Since she and Frank had traveled so often, her living style had been incredibly minimalistic, which suited not only the owner of a rambunctious cat but also someone moving into a tiny apartment.

The woman positioned herself behind the main counter adjacent to the front door. She situated a heater to blow hot air at her legs since it was easier for the men to prop open the front door. Several of her shop neighbors came by to say hello and wish her well. But they left quickly every time a large piece of furniture or armload of boxes was carried past.

She had just finished setting up the new banking accounts on her computer when another shadow fell across her face and keyboard.

"You're much more approachable when you aren't armed," said a familiar, smooth voice. Dorothy started and looked up into Destin Hollanday's smiling face.

Dorothy narrowed her eyes. "Can I help you?"

Destin continued to smile. He removed his hat and ran his hand over his slick-backed hair. "I wanted to see how you were settling in. And to see if you had given my offer anymore thought."

"If you believe I have any intention of leaving here to go gallivanting across the globe, you have the wrong horse and pony, Mr. Hollanday." Dorothy made a show of shuffling through a stack of paperwork beside her. Destin's smile was becoming more annoying by the moment.

"Why not? You used to do it all the time," he said.

Dorothy pulled a folder from the middle of the stack and watched a cascade of receipts fall out and onto the floor. "I was retired," she snipped, pushing the heater aside to pick up the papers on the floor.

"So that's your excuse," Destin said from above her.

"It is not an excuse!" Dorothy cried from beneath the counter. She pushed herself up and smacked her head on the edge of the counter. "It is not an excuse."

"You're afraid," said Destin. "It's completely understandable. Felix kept everything secret, which would be required of you as well."

Dorothy glowered across the counter at Destin. One hand clutched the fallen receipts, the other massaging the bump forming on her head. "My father's name was Richard, Mr. Destin. Whatever secrets he kept, he took with him to the grave, and that, sir, is where they will stay."

"Except the scroll, correct?"

Dorothy looked up from the computer she had been attempting to distract herself with. She swallowed and stuck her chin out. "I don't know what you're talking about."

"The Auritean texts. You sent the artifact to your friend yesterday after our conversation."

Dorothy opened her mouth, but no words would come. Destin held up a hand.

"Please, do not alarm yourself, Ms. Claes. It's all right. Your father did the same with many of his colleagues. Let me know when she calls." He smirked again.

"Mr. Hollanday, I have work I need to attend to. I don't have time to entertain your little fantasies."

Destin nodded and picked up his hat from the end of the counter. "Yes, I can imagine taking over Felix's shop unexpectedly must be a task. My apologies. But when you're ready for a break…" He pushed a large envelope across the counter to her. "Please, call me anytime."

He slid past one of the movers as they entered and disappeared up the street. Dorothy watched him go, her cheeks still flush with confusion.

An hour later, the men had placed the last of the boxes on the top landing. She quickly inspected their work, then ushered them more curtly than she'd intended out of the shop. She turned the sign on the door to Closed and locked the deadbolt.

Upstairs, Solomon zoomed around the apartment, leaping from table to chair and back again. Dorothy sat in her own armchair, which she had positioned in front of the little cast-iron stove. She watched the flames flicker in its belly and clutched the envelope in her hand. The cat meowed at her feet and wound himself around her ankles. He sniffed the envelope and batted at it. When he finally jumped into the woman's lap and licked her chin, she sighed and stroked his jet-black fur. He settled onto her leg, kneading his claws gently into her knee.

Dorothy looked at the envelope, her hands beginning to tremble. Across the front were the words Classified. Silver Foxes. Cats in silver text. Dorothy removed the clasp and opened the flap. A strange series of documents poured out and onto Solomon's back. He meowed and turned to catch the corner of a picture in his teeth.

"Leave it," Dorothy scolded. Solomon released the picture and went back to grooming his paw.

The pictures appeared to be of a cat show. Rows of cages filled with cat breeds from across the world lined the hall. Stacks of papers with scores and divisions were paper-clipped together, and a list of names written in red pen was attached to the back.

"Cats disappear from cages. No memory from judges or owners. Records of scoring and lineage always found," said one of the notes.

Dorothy leaned forward on her elbows and read each piece of paper start to finish. It wasn't until Solomon dropped one of his jingle balls loudly into his food dish did she realize how much time had passed. She gathered up the paperwork and stuffed it back into the envelope. Solomon meowed excitedly as Dorothy pulled a tin of canned food from a box on the counter. She dumped the foul-smelling pate into the bowl and stroked the cat absentmindedly.

A secret organization. A mysterious scroll. Disappearing cats. Dorothy shook her head. Even the Greeks couldn't have made up this sort of thing. She headed to bed and spent the next several hours tossing and turning, her mind unwilling to rest and Solomon blissfully pouncing on her feet.

FOUR

THE GLOWING ANTIQUE LIGHTS FLICKERED above Dorothy's head. A heavy snowfall had been forecasted for the day, but the swell had shifted north, turning into an outright blizzard. Dorothy had called Aaron before he'd even been out of bed. She had gathered from his sleepy voice that he had heard and understood enough not to come into the shop that day. After that, she took the opportunity to explore more of the strange basement beyond the bookcase passage.

The center of the room was lined with hip-high, scrubbed wooden tables. Each held an odd assortment of artifacts preserved beneath a glass case, including the ones Destin had shown her. An ancient mask, like those seen during Día de Muertos, stared up at Dorothy. A golden plaque in front of it read, "Ecuador, 1987. Case # UNSF031087054."

An intricate piece of tapestry lay beneath a sheet of glass, embedded into the table itself. It was over six feet long. Dorothy's heart skipped a beat when she noticed familiar colorations and figures. Could it be the missing piece of the Bayeux Tapestry? This one had a golden plaque as well that read, "Normandy, 1992. Case # UNSF112492115."

Dorothy sighed and leaned against the wooden table. Thanksgiving 1992. Her father had been called away on a business trip just days before. He had said there was a priceless antique that the buyer needed to sell immediately. He had promised to return before Dorothy's mother carved the turkey. And he had kept to his word. Richard Van Damme had bounced through the door carrying a sack in one arm like a modern-day Santa Claus just as Mrs. Van Damme had raised the carving knife to the bird.

Dorothy found a chair and sank into it, her hand finding its way to her mouth. This must have been what he had left for. But why would he not have notified someone that he had discovered the rest of the Bayeux Tapestry? It had quietly sat beneath a pane of glass, under her very feet for nearly a quarter of a century. Richard Van Damme had indeed held more secrets than his family ever could have imagined.

Solomon came flying down the hall and dashed

through the open doorway. He meowed and jumped onto Dorothy's lap, rubbing his face into her so hard, he smacked the top of his head sharply against her jaw. Dorothy smiled and scratched between his ears.

"You're so silly," she cooed at him. The cat shoved his whiskers up her nose and the woman kissed the top of his head. "Come on. It's getting cold down here." She headed back up the winding stone stair and shut the bookcase behind her. Solomon had barely cleared the little sitting room to the landing by the stairs when a phone began to ring.

Dorothy righted the Silver Foxes book and hurried to the old rotary phone.

"Hello?" she said, a bit of concern in her voice. She wasn't expecting any phone calls, but a storm this size always led to injuries. Folk trying to walk to the store down the street and getting hit by a wayward car. A gust of wind pushing someone into a ditch, where they would sit trapped until help could be called.

"Dorothy?" It was Dorothy's sister.

"Mary Pat?" The worry in Dorothy's voice heightened. "Are you all right? Is Jimmy all right?"

"Oh, of course we're fine, Dory-dear. You know I was just so worried about Dad living all alone up there in that tiny little loft. And now that you're there, and what with the storm and all…"

Dorothy collapsed into the chair beside the phone, holding her head in her free hand. "Mary Pat, did your cable go out?" She immediately pulled the receiver away from her ear, waiting for her sister's high-pitched reply.

"Oh! My goodness, I guess it did. You know, with this storm, I suppose it was bound to happen. It's amazing the phones haven't –"

"Mary Pat?" Dorothy rubbed her fingers together in front of the mouthpiece. "I-I can't hear you."

"Dorothy?"

"I think the phones are –" Dorothy hit the button on the base and disconnected the call with a chuckle.

She looked up and saw Solomon staring at her from atop her father's desk.

"What? Would you prefer I entertain my big sister for three hours until she runs out of gossip?"

Solomon trilled, turned in a circle, and settled down to lick his paw. The woman smiled at him. She made to move from the chair, but her back and knees were suddenly very stiff. She rubbed at the side of her leg, cursing the cold stone floor of the basement. She had to have been down there for hours. She had hoped to find paperwork that would explain how the strange artifacts had come to be in her father's possession. But there had been nothing.

After a few moments, Dorothy pushed herself from the chair. She groaned, her body cracking and popping in a way that would rival any puffed rice cereal. She set a kettle to boil, then began studying the books in the bookcase.

Perhaps any documents had been stored in a hollow book or another secret little box the bookcase would reveal. She picked up the first book on the top shelf and opened it carefully. It was an old arithmetic book, much like what her father would have used in school as a child. She turned each page with delicate fingers until she reached the end. Nothing.

The next book was from the late 1800s called The Dryad. It was in nearly pristine condition. Dorothy forced herself not to get lost in the intricate prose of a bygone era, but by the time she reached the end of that book as well, she had still come up empty-handed.

The kettle whistled behind her and Solomon rushed to sit at the base of the cast iron stove, looking expectantly up at the rising steam. He stared wide-eyed, watching the steam disappear a few feet above the kettle.

"I suppose I'll never know the truth about Dad's secrets," Dorothy whispered, setting another book back on the shelf. She reached into the kitchenette cabinet and pulled out a ceramic teacup. Solomon walked in a circle, still not taking his eyes off the steam. He meowed at it and likely would have swiped a paw at the rising condensation if he could reach. He didn't understand, but it did not stop his curiosity.

Dorothy poured the hot liquid over her tea strainer. She moved to sit in her armchair again when she heard an antique phone ring somewhere in the distance. Solomon's ears perked up, and he looked from the bookcase to the steam and back again. In an instant, Dorothy realized it was the phone in her the basement. She set the cup of tea on her end table and rushed to pull the Silver Fox book in the bookcase. Her knees ached as she rushed down the winding stair and threw open the heavy door.

"Hello?" she said into the receiver, breathless.

"Goodness, Ms. Claes, I would have waited," came Destin Hollanday's patient voice.

"Mr. Hollanday." Dorothy's knees hurt even more, but somehow, she felt it was more from her annoyance with this man than anything else. "What can I do for you this evening? Surely, you have better things to do in a January blizzard than bother the likes of me."

"I do apologize for the inconvenience, Ms. Claes, however, if you have no intention of carrying on your father's work, now is the time for me to arrange the transport of those artifacts. Due to their sensitive nature, such a thing is best done under cover of dark, and snow for that matter. I assume you have read the case file I gave you?"

"Yes," said Dorothy. Her heart was pounding. He wanted to take her father's artifacts?

"The case is very active, as I'm sure you read. We suspect the next incident to occur in Paris next weekend. If you are not interested in the case –"

"I never said I wasn't," Dorothy quipped, and she immediately regretted it. She could practically hear Destin's smirk curling the corners of his mouth. Her face flushed just thinking about it.

"Excellent. I will have Artie arrange your flight and passport. And Solomon as well. I do believe he will make a fine show cat. Someone will be in touch with you soon. I recommend you arrange for Aaron to cover the shop while you are away. He is quite accustomed to it, you will find. He's a good lad. Good night, Ms. Claes."

"I never said –"

There was a loud click, and the phone went quiet. Dorothy blinked into the darkness of the room, stunned at what had just occurred. Solomon rubbed against her leg and meowed excitedly. She set the receiver back on its base and lifted the cat into her arms.

"I suppose this means we're heading to Paris, *mon chat*."

FIVE

"I HAVE A BUYER COMING IN FOR THOSE glass door knobs in the case. I told him $130, and not a penny less. The invoice is written up in the folder next to the register. Make sure you run the vacuum by the door before you go. I don't want the salt from the sidewalks damaging the carpet. And please email Mr. Johnston about getting that list for the auction next month. He hasn't gotten back to me."

"I can handle it, Ms. Claes," Aaron replied kindly to Dorothy. "Richard used to leave the shop in my care quite frequently. I promise I will call if anything happens." He smiled at her, then picked up the ball Solomon had deposited at his feet and rolled it down the walkway.

Dorothy nodded. "Yes, you're right. I'm sorry."

"No worries, ma'am." The young man picked up a

box on the counter between them and headed into a back room to sort and catalog their latest inventory purchases.

Dorothy sighed as she watched him go, Solomon trotting behind him with his ball in his mouth. She had spent the last five days researching cat shows and brushing up on her French. She had been thankful for the blizzard, and for Aaron. She had barely done a lick of work for the antique shop since her arrival nearly a week ago. The place was in serious need of dusting, and Solomon had somehow gotten paw and nose prints all over the front window. But that would have to wait.

Her bags had been packed since the night Destin had called her, and she had even taken Solomon to the vet to update his health record for the plane ride. But the antique phone in the basement had been eerily quiet. By now, Dorothy could name every breed accepted by the Cat Fanciers Organization. She knew the regional director by sight, as well as all six judges that would be present at the show that weekend. She had even dug up as much as she could find on the five suspects the Foxes had targeted.

But the investigation was not her main focus. She knew those artifacts had something to do with her father's death, and she needed them to discover the truth. If Destin Hollanday wasn't going to tell her, then she would have to find out for herself. If he had been targeted, poisoned or killed due to his involvement with the Silver Foxes, his killer might still be out there. Dorothy Virginia Shirley Claes was not about to let her father's possible killer go free.

She heard the front door open and looked up. Two women bundled up in several layers of coats, hats and gloves entered. One removed her fur hat and large, dark sunglasses with glorious exuberance. "My, it hasn't changed a bit, has it?"

"It's barely been a month, Kitty," the other woman replied. She was plump with short, cropped black hair. Everything she wore was beautiful and brightly colored.

"May I help you, ladies?" Dorothy called to them.

The first woman squealed with delight when her eyes landed on Dorothy. She glided across the room with such grace, she looked like she was floating.

"Dorothy," she said airily, "it is such a pleasure to meet you." The woman held out her hand and Dorothy saw her nails had been professionally painted with little snowflakes and a snowman on the thumb. She shook the first woman's hand as the second approached.

"I'm sorry. Do I know you?"

"Destin sent us," said the second woman. She gave a wink and pointed to a silver pin on the collar of her jacket. It was a fox. Dorothy suppressed a gasp. "He wanted us to deliver this to you."

The plump woman handed Dorothy a small packet of papers. She opened the top piece and saw her passport.

"Fanny D. Fennec?" she read aloud. "This – this isn't right."

"We haven't had a Fanny Fennec for years," the first woman said. She leaned nonchalantly against the counter. "If I remember correctly, our last Fanny was at least fifty years ago."

"It's good to see more women in the foxes." The second woman nodded her head in agreement. She looked at Dorothy and continued. "Felix was an absolute gem of a man, but I've always believed us women have more of a knack for this sort of thing."

"It's the socializing part. We're more natural at the small talk," the first woman added with a casual nod.

Dorothy stared dumbfounded at the two women as Solomon suddenly came rushing out of the back room, meowing and purring as he ran. The first woman leaned against the counter as he approached, but the second stooped to pet him.

"This must be our little honorary spy," she cooed at

the cat. Solomon meowed back as though in agreement and accepted her pets and scratches with enthusiasm.

"Hmm, yes. I'm not much of a cat person myself. Probably why Destin didn't assign me, after all. Though my French is impeccable."

Solomon jumped onto the counter, and Dorothy collected the cat in her arms, taking a protective step back.

"I believe I've missed something," she replied. "I am not Fanny, and my father's name was Richard."

"It's your code name, sweetheart," the first woman whispered.

"My name is Kitty. My code name is Kit Fox. And this is Caprice. Her code is Cape Fox."

Dorothy raised an eyebrow at them. "But my name is not Fanny," she said again.

The woman named Caprice smiled. "And mine is not Caprice. It's for your own protection, dear. And ours."

"We only know your name because of Felix. These sorts of things aren't generally handed down between families." Kitty had pulled a manicure pick from her pocket and was digging at something under her nail.

"If you know my name, then why don't you just call me Dorothy?" She raised an eyebrow at the women, who both exchanged a look and shrugged.

"Dorothy it is," said Caprice.

"Oh! I nearly forgot!" Kitty quickly dug around in her designer handbag. She caught Dorothy staring as she did so. "Do you like it?" She stopped looking for whatever she had remembered and lifted the bag onto the counter. "It's one of my favorite designs of the season."

"Kitty is a fashion designer."

Kitty waved her hand at Caprice. "Oh, sweetheart, I am the fashion designer of Louisiana. Christian Dior doesn't have an off-the-shoulder sweater on me!" She resumed digging in her bag until she produced a tiny fox pin. The stripe across its tail was made of brass.

"The boys get little cuff links," she said and handed the pin to Dorothy. "Luckily, we get to be a bit more fashionable. I added the bit of brass as a nod to Felix and the shop. Do you like it?" She stared at Dorothy with such hope and enthusiasm, Dorothy couldn't help but grin. She set Solomon on the counter and accepted the pin.

"It's lovely," she replied.

Kitty squealed again. "Oh, I'm so glad you like it!"

"Miss Kitty?" came Aaron's voice from the back room. He wheeled his chair toward the door and leaned out to look at the two ladies.

"Hello, Aaron." Caprice waved at Aaron, who

beamed and jumped up from his chair.

"Miss Caprice," he said, giving a small bow to the women.

"Oh, Aaron, you're such a sweetie," cooed Kitty.

"We came to offer our respects to Ms. Claes and introduce ourselves," Caprice said as she nodded toward Dorothy.

"Miss Kitty and Miss Caprice were some of Richard's colleagues. They helped him acquire several antiques from around the world."

"Indeed," said Dorothy. She and Caprice exchanged smiles.

Solomon had begun inching closer to Kitty, who was hurriedly backing away from the counter.

"Well, I believe we should be going." Kitty pulled on her velvet gloves and carefully placed her hat around her delicate bun and braid. "It was so wonderful to meet you, Fan – Dorothy. Good luck on your trip." She nodded at the cat, who had tried to paw at her, and took off for the front door.

"If you need anything, our contacts are in the paperwork," said Caprice. She shook Dorothy's hand and hugged Aaron before joining Kitty at the door.

Dorothy watched them go and chuckled when Kitty nearly slipped on the snow in her high-heeled leather boots.

"Miss Kitty takes a bit to get to used to," said Aaron, also watching as the women disappeared around the corner together. "But she's a lovely lady."

"And Caprice?" Dorothy asked him.

"Miss Caprice is a tour guide in the Cape Peninsula. She has the most fascinating stories. I could listen to her for hours."

"Hmm," said Dorothy. "Well, we don't have hours, unfortunately." She sifted through the stack of paperwork the women had given her. She found a new health certificate for Solomon listing a Fanny Fennec as the owner. Dorothy shook her head and continued digging until she found her flight schedule. She glanced at her watch and her eyes widened.

"Four hours!" she cried. "Aaron, will you please call a cab to pick me up here in an hour?"

"Yes, ma'am," he said, heading for the back room again.

"Oh, Aaron!" Dorothy called. "Make sure you eat lunch while you're here. I won't have you starving yourself all day."

Aaron smirked and nodded. "Yes, ma'am."

Dorothy lugged her suitcase from the trunk of the

taxi. She picked up Solomon's carrier and nodded her appreciation to the driver before heading toward the main building of the tiny airport. At first, she questioned whether she was in the right location at all. The building was adjacent to a military base she hadn't even known was there.

The woman at the counter smiled when she entered. "How may I help you?" she asked.

Dorothy took a tentative look around. A few military personnel sat in chairs along the far wall staring at their phones. No one else was in the room. Solomon gave a meow of protest that echoed throughout the room, causing the military staff to look up. The old woman hushed him and handed the concierge a booklet of papers.

"Ah, Ms. Fennec. Yes, Artie is waiting for you. Right this way." She slid her security card through a reader beside a glass door. It clicked, and she held it open for Dorothy. Solomon meowed pitifully again as Dorothy headed through the door. They walked along a carpeted hall. The woman stopped at another secure door, this one thicker and made of metal.

It opened into a small aircraft hangar. The woman held the door for Dorothy and smiled as she stepped through.

"Enjoy your flight," she said, closing the door

behind her.

"Wait!" Dorothy called, but the woman had already gone.

A small business jet sat in the center of the hangar. Its windows were dark, and the door closed. Dorothy took a cautious step forward, her shoes clicking on the concrete floor.

"Hello?" she said into the darkness. She approached the jet but saw no one. Then the door to the main cabin opened. The smiling face of a man appeared in the doorway. He leapt to the floor with surprising ease considering the stark whiteness of his hair, and the weather-worn wrinkles in his face. As she studied him more closely, she recognized him as the man who had given her father bunny ears in the picture from Destin.

"Ms. Fennec," he said politely, holding out a hand to her. Dorothy shook his hand, feeling the rough calluses of someone who was unafraid of hard work.

"It's Dorothy," the woman corrected him.

The man nodded. "Artie, your pilot for this mission. Welcome aboard." He pulled a set of steps from beneath the plane and offered out a hand for Solomon's carrier. The woman swallowed and handed the carrier to the pilot before ascending the steps.

Inside, the plane was simple but clean. Glasses of water and tumblers for whiskey sat in a small compartment along the row of windows. On one of the seats sat a plush cat bed in royal purple velvet with emerald and silver trim. A large 'S' had been embroidered in the center of the pillow, and neatly folded beside the pillow were a set of matching curtains and drapes for the cat show cage. Dorothy set Solomon's carrier on one of the seats and opened the door for him. He bounded across the seats and immediately curled up on the velvet pillow, purring madly and kneading at the soft fabric. Dorothy found a note tucked in the folds of the curtains. From Miss Kitty, it read.

"We'll be taking off soon," Artie said from behind them. "He'll need to be in his carrier at least until we're in the air."

Dorothy nodded as Artie headed back down the steps. She heard him collapse the stairs back beneath the plane and shut the door. She turned to Solomon, her heart beginning to pound in her chest. She hadn't been out of the country since Frank had passed. If only he could see her now. He would have jumped at the chance for such an adventure. Come to think of it, Dorothy knew she would have too – three years ago, anyway. Solomon stood on his pillow, pawing at the fabric and staring at Dorothy. His tail gently waved back and forth. He lifted a paw in the air and extended his claws at Dorothy.

She heard a door open and close in the cockpit area at the front of the plane. She scooped Solomon back into his carrier and buckled them both into the white leather seats. The engines whirred to life, and the plane began to move. The hangar outside the windows became blinding bright as the main door opened.

"We're taxiing to the runway now, Ms. Fennec. We'll be in the air in just a few moments," Artie's voice said over the intercom system. Dorothy nodded, more to herself than the pilot, who couldn't see her anyway. She watched as the plane maneuvered onto the runway, and then as the trees and runway lights sped by the window faster and faster. She barely felt the plane lift into the air, its only indication of ascent that the tops of the trees were now eye level.

When the plane had leveled out, the little light over the cockpit door that read Fasten Your Safety Belts switched off. Dorothy immediately threw off her belt and opened Solomon's cage door. She began rummaging in the cabinet beneath the water glasses, looking desperately for the whiskey. Whatever she had gotten herself into, there was no turning back now.

"We appear to have clear skies for most of the way, Ms. Fennec. You should arrive safely at your destination in about twelve hours. There are drinks and hors-d'oeuvres in the cabinet. Please enjoy your flight."

Dorothy looked out the window and watched as the clouds passed beneath her, the ocean coming closer and closer. Solomon jumped from his pillow and set his paws on the glass, watching the cars passing like a little toy scene below them. Dorothy threw back a swallow of whiskey and settled into the soft chair to sleep.

It was the whirring of an electronic gear that woke Dorothy. She looked up and saw a small panel had unfolded from the ceiling above the cockpit door. Artie's face illuminated the screen. He tapped on the headset he was wearing and pointed to a compartment beside Dorothy's chair. She opened it and found an identical headset. She hurriedly put it on and, fighting Solomon, plugged in the little cord to the plane's private intercom system.

"Can you hear me, Ms. Fennec?" Artie asked.

"Yes," Dorothy replied.

"Good. This is a secure channel, and I can now debrief you on your assignment. You will find more documentation in the compartment beside you."

Dorothy reached over and pulled out another envelope much like the first that Destin had given her.

"You will arrive in Paris in five hours. I apologize for the confusion. Another plane joined us partway across the Atlantic and will be our decoy plane."

"Decoy plane?" Dorothy asked.

Artie nodded. "There are many, both within and outside the UN, who would like nothing more than to get their hands on the artifacts the Silver Foxes are in charge of neutralizing. Both war and peace would be possible in a single day with such pieces of history."

"If you have the ability to bring about world peace, then why wouldn't you?" Dorothy snapped.

"Politics, dear Fennec. The answer to everything in this world is not, in fact, forty-two, but politics."

Dorothy went red and sighed.

"Nevertheless, it is my job to brief you on your mission. Have you memorized the names from the file?"

"Yes, there were five," replied Dorothy.

"There are only three now. Two of our suspects have canceled their reservations with the hotel and show. Other agents are investigating them at this time. Your three remaining targets are Karen Augusta, Jeff Martin, and Sharon Rhors."

"Karen's one of the judges," said Dorothy. She opened the envelope and pulled out the paper with Karen's information.

"And she has several friends who show their cats. Her motive would be to help her friends earn more points, and thus be able to sell their pedigree cats for more money. She could be getting a kickback."

"Jeff is the regional director for the west coast," Dorothy continued pulling out the man's information sheet.

"And he is up for reelection in three months. One of his competitors was a recent victim at one of the cat shows in Wisconsin. It could be a way to eliminate his competition."

"Hmm," Dorothy mused. She slid Jeff's paper behind Karen's, revealing Sharon Rhors.

"Sharon is from Paris?" Dorothy asked, reading the woman's bio.

Artie nodded. "That's why we are sending you to this show. We believe if Sharon is the culprit, then this is where we can catch her."

"Sharon's a breeder, and in the program to become a judge."

"Sharon also owns one of only three breeds of cats who have yet to be affected by whatever is causing this. She is our number one suspect."

A small plastic bag fell onto Dorothy's lap. Solomon immediately jumped up to sniff and investigate it. Dorothy snatched the bag away before the cat could carry it off.

"Those are GPS trackers. You'll find another bag as well. These are voice recorders. Friday, you'll set up your cage in the show hall. Take this opportunity to meet everyone if you can. Saturday is day one of the show. You will need to find a way to place one of the GPS trackers and one of the audio recorders on each of your targets. Sharon is, of course, your number one priority."

"And how am I supposed to do that?" Dorothy stared at Artie intently through the little screen.

Artie shrugged. "This is your mission, lady fox. I suppose Destin would say something about improvising with style. Your father, on the other hand, was more of the social connoisseur. Make friends, Ms. Fennec. Make friends and trust no one. Remember, this isn't a game. The United Nations is counting on you to neutralize whatever this artifact is. This could be a testing ground for something far more sinister. If world leaders began disappearing with no one remembering who they were, absolute and utter chaos would ensue. Even if our governments refuse to bring about world peace, the last thing they want is its destruction. If you need anything from me, push the little button beside your chair there. It will activate the screen. Good luck, Ms. Fennec."

The screen went black and slowly folded back up into the ceiling. Dorothy grabbed her tumbler of whiskey and threw back another shot. This Fennec name was getting completely out of hand.

Six

PARIS, FRANCE HAD BEEN ONE OF THE FIRST cities Dorothy and Frank had moved to after they'd retired. Or rather, a tiny apartment in Fontenay-sous-Bois, a small commune in the eastern suburbs of Paris. The apartment had barely been six hundred square feet, but Dorothy had loved it. It had a tiny trellis balcony that was just large enough for two little chairs. It overlooked a tiny garden in the center square below, and in the distance, Paris had spread out before them.

The taxi dropped Dorothy and Solomon at their hotel. It was just after midnight, and the city was still bustling. It was barely 8 p.m. in Lexington, but both woman and cat were exhausted. She fell onto the hotel bed, Solomon snuggling on the pillow beside her as the two fell into a deep slumber.

The show hall didn't open until later that afternoon.

Dorothy woke before dawn and slipped Solomon's leash and harness on. It had been years since she had roamed the streets of Paris with Frank. But if her memory still served her, there was a small pastry shop only a few blocks from the hotel.

The two padded down the now-quiet streets. The little black cat led the way, his tail happily swaying back and forth, and the older woman following, her eyes darting skeptically into every dark corner. The smell of freshly baking pastries from Bon Appétit Beignet wafted down the street and met Dorothy's nose before she had even found the shop. She smiled and closed her eyes, thinking of grabbing Frank's hand in hers. Instead, Solomon's leash gave a tug as he darted up the street. One of the bakers had just turned on the lights and unlocked the door. He smiled when he saw the cat press his nose and front paws against the pane of glass. He opened the door and greeted the cat with a scratch behind the ears.

"Vous avez bon goût en patisserie, petit chat," said the man as they entered. You have good taste in pastry, little cat.

"Oui," Dorothy replied. "Do you have any of those breakfast pastries anymore?" Her French was still a little rusty, but the man seemed to understand.

"Of course," he replied in English this time. "And

what for our little chat noir? Ah, a pork and cheese soufflé!" The man lifted a part of the counter on a hinge and busied himself with arranging a tiny soufflé tart on a ceramic plate for Solomon. He did the same for Dorothy and served them both at a little table by the window. The sun was just beginning to turn the sky from black to gray. A young couple snuck out of a back alley, then pressed themselves against the brick building, kissing and embracing each other before going their separate ways.

"Doux amour. To be young and in love," the man said.

"To be old and in love is just as sweet," Dorothy said before winking at the man. He laughed and returned to his place behind the counter as another customer entered.

"Sharon Rhors," said the woman to the baker. Dorothy's head snapped around. Standing at the counter was a middle-aged woman, her smooth red hair flowing down the back of a bright red coat.

"Ah, le croquembouche, oui?" the man asked.

The woman nodded. The baker disappeared in back, and Sharon turned to smile at Dorothy. Her eyes fell on Solomon and her face brightened.

"Oh, que c'est mignon!" she cried. *How cute!* "Puis-je?" *May I?* She held out her hand to the cat, who

promptly turned from his soufflé and rubbed his head on the woman's hand.

"We are attending the cat show this weekend," Dorothy said in her best French, which was still a bit broken. "It's our first time."

"Oh, that's wonderful!" Sharon replied in perfect English. "I'm actually a breeder myself. I will be attending as well. Did you fly here all the way from America?"

"*Oui*, er... yes. We were visiting for vacation and I thought it would be fun." Dorothy's stomach dropped. She hopped the flush she felt in her cheeks at lying wasn't too obvious to Sharon.

"Well, we are so happy to have you. Here's my card. I'll be showing the Egyptian Maus. If you need anything, please do not hesitate to ask. Are you coming this afternoon to set up?" Sharon handed Dorothy a business card, and a beaded bracelet slipped from beneath the cuff of her jacket. Dorothy eyed it, remembering the strange artifacts in her father's basement.

"Sorry?" Dorothy asked her.

"The show doesn't start until tomorrow, but most of us are setting up this afternoon. I would love to invite you to dinner with my friends after if you aren't already busy."

"Madam," the shop owner called from behind them. Sharon and Dorothy turned to see a tower of pastry balls piled high on a golden stand.

"Croquembouche is one of my favorites," Sharon whispered as she flashed an excited smile. "I'll see you tonight. *Au revoir, mes amis!*" She gave Solomon one last scratch on the head and bent to kiss Dorothy on her cheek.

Dorothy watched as Sharon and the shop owner fawned over the tower of dough balls and caramel. They carefully packed it into a tall box, and Sharon waved as she turned to leave. She opened the door and nearly collided with a gray-haired man.

"Oh, Jeffery," Sharon said a bit awkwardly, her hand flying to her heart.

"Sharon," Jeff Martin replied curtly. His eyes narrowed as he stared at the package in the woman's hands.

"You startled me." Sharon gave a nervous laugh and shifted the box in her grip.

"My apologies." Jeff pushed past Sharon and approached the counter.

Sharon passed a nervous glance at Dorothy. She tried to look away, but Sharon had already caught her eye.

"We have a newcomer to our show this weekend."

Sharon's sweet demeanor had returned. Jeff glanced over his shoulder at Sharon but did not reply. Sharon closed the door she had been holding open and walked back to Dorothy and Solomon. "This is... I'm sorry," Sharon giggled. "I didn't even catch your name."

Dorothy hesitated, remembering her undercover agent name. "Dorothy," she said. "My name is Dorothy Fennec." It wasn't a complete lie.

Sharon smiled. "Jeff, this is Dorothy. She's visiting from the States this weekend."

Jeff turned from the counter and stared from Sharon to Dorothy and back again. Reluctantly, he approached and held out a hand to Dorothy.

"Nice to have some good American blood around here," he said, not bothering to hide the side glance he shot at Sharon.

"It's good to meet you," said Dorothy. "This is Solomon."

At the mention of his name, the cat placed his front paws on the table and pushed his head into Sharon's elbow. The woman stepped back to allow Jeff a chance at petting the cat. But Jeff, too, had shifted. He and Sharon collided, and the bottom of the pastry box split open. The tower of croquembouche collapsed to the floor, shattering into a mass of beautiful, fluffy dough and broken caramel strings.

"Oh, non! Non! Mon croquembouche! Qu'est-il arrivé?" the shop owner called, his voice ringing with utter devastation.

Sharon, Jeff, and the shop owner began speaking very quickly in French. Dorothy was left forgotten behind them. She pulled Solomon back as he tried to sneak a piece of pastry that lay on the floor beneath his chair.

Sharon was crying now, and the shop owner was attempting to comfort her, though he looked on the verge of tears himself. After several minutes, Jeff left the shop with a single scone, and Sharon had left empty-handed.

Dorothy stood, returning the two ceramic plates to the counter as the shopkeeper disappeared to find a broom. Solomon pawed at her pant leg and gave a pitiful meow. Dorothy watched as the man reappeared. Make friends, Artie had said. "And trust no one," she mumbled to herself, pulling out her credit card.

"Excusez-moi," Dorothy said. "I would like to place an order for a croquembouche, please."

$\mathscr{S}$EVEN

DOROTHY LEFT SOLOMON SCRATCHING AT their hotel room door. She loaded one of the hotel carts and rolled it through the hallways to the attached conference hall. When she opened the door, a sea of colored show cages and cats spread before her. Fluffy Ragdolls with pink satin and lace trimmed curtains. Chocolate and lilac Burmese in a golden show cage. Even naked Sphinxes wrapped in fleece sweaters.

She stopped in the doorway, completely awed.

"Puis-je vous aider?" someone asked from behind her.

"Pardon?" Dorothy turned, her eyes still wide.

"May I help you?" the woman asked again in English. She wore a crochet sweater with tiny pom-poms sewn in the shape of two kittens playing with a ball of yarn.

"I'm-I'm Dorothy. I'm new," she spluttered.

The woman's scowl immediately brightened. "Ah, welcome, *mon amie!* Come! Come!" She placed a hand on Dorothy's shoulder and led her through the door. People stared as she walked by, pushing the hotel cart before her. "I have you by Karlee. She's been with us for about a year. She'll be delighted she's no longer the new girl."

A short, young girl with bright pink hair stood beside an empty table. She ran a brush through her cat's coat and spoke softly to it. She had to have been in her early twenties, and she sported the typical skinny jeans and hoodie of her generation. She was a little hipster from head to toe, save for the Egyptian cat pendant she wore around her neck.

"Karlee," said the woman to the girl. Karlee pulled a pair of earbuds from her ears and looked up with large blue eyes. "This is Dorothy. She's new."

Karlee practically squealed with delight. "Oh, it's so great to meet you! I'll show you everything – don't worry," she said as she began bouncing on the balls of her feet. The woman patted Dorothy's arm and walked away, much to Dorothy's surprise.

"So, what kind of cat do you have?" Karlee asked before zipping her show cage closed. She also spoke perfect English, and Dorothy remembered most children in Europe were raised bilingual.

"Solomon's not a purebred," said Dorothy, waving her hand before her. Karlee reached under the empty bench and pulled out a wire cage. She began assembling it as she spoke.

"Oh, household pets and rescues are my favorite." Karlee giggled, her little dimples becoming more prominent. "Though I say that about almost all the breeds. Do you have cage curtains?"

Dorothy reached into the bag on the hotel cart and pulled out the cage curtains and pillow Kitty had made. Karlee gasped, running her hand over the plush, purple velvet.

"Oh. Mon. Dieu. This is amazing! Did you make this?"

"Ah, no. My friend made it for me. I am not that talented."

Karlee tossed the curtains over the wire cage and arranged the fabric delicately. She set the pillow on one side of the cage and pulled a catnip mouse from her bag, laying it on the pillow.

"There," she said. "Perfect!"

Dorothy smiled her thanks. The young girl reminded her of her great-nephew, Mary Pat's eldest grandson, Ricky. He had the same bubbly and carefree attitude. She was sure the two would have been friends, and

Dorothy felt an immediate fondness for the young girl. She pulled her attention away from Karlee's breathless giddiness and began looking around the show hall.

"Here." Karlee hooked her arm through Dorothy's and pulled her to the end of the aisle. "Let me introduce you to everyone."

Most of the judges and their clerks were setting up in their rings. Karlee smiled and waved at each judge as they passed, leading Dorothy from one person to another for introductions.

"And what breed are you showing, Ms. Fennec?" one judge asked.

"She's got a household pet," Karlee answered for her. Dorothy simply smiled and nodded.

"*Ah, oui!* Most of our breeders started with rescue cats. Have you considered a pedigree?"

"I am quite certain Solomon is more than enough for me right now," Dorothy said, holding up both hands.

The judge laughed. "I understand. And you were working on getting an Egyptian Mau, is that correct, Karlee?"

"My fiancé, Scott, wants to be involved in picking one out. I'm waiting for him to get back from his internship."

The judge nodded. "Well, you know I love a good

Mau. Let me know if I can help you. And Ms. Fennec, it was wonderful to meet you. Good luck tomorrow."

Karlee led Dorothy away, then almost immediately squealed with delight again. She jumped up and down, Dorothy still attached to her arm.

"Karen!" Karlee finally unhooked herself from Dorothy and ran toward an elderly judge who had just arrived. Dorothy recognized her as Karen Augusta. She smiled when she saw Karlee kiss the woman on the cheek in greeting.

"Karlee!" Karen welcomed her. "I didn't know you were going to be here," the judge said. She set her bag on the judging table and began unpacking. She pulled out a small, stuffed cat and set it gently beside her stack of papers.

"How's your family?" Karlee asked, nodding at the little cat.

"We are as well as can be expected," Karen answered. "Benjamin's mother has only just begun packing up the nursery. But she gave me back the little cat I had given him when he was born." Karen picked up the stuffed cat and gave it a small hug before setting it back on the table.

She looked up and smiled sadly at Karlee. The girl set a hand on her arm. The woman's eyes shifted and widened.

"Oh! Is this the necklace Scott bought for you?" Karen asked, her tone completely changed.

Karlee touched the pendant around her neck, and it made a soft rattling, as though there were beads inside.

"Yeah. He bought it for me in Cairo while he was there. Now he sends me these little cat statues whenever I go to a show. He's so sweet."

There was a moment of silence as Karen seemed lost in her thoughts, staring at the necklace around Karlee's neck. Finally, the girl broke the silence. "Oh, this is Dorothy. She's from the States and visiting us. This is her first show!" Karlee beamed at Dorothy, who forced her eyes away from the stuffed cat and smiled awkwardly.

"Nice to meet you," Karen said and shook Dorothy's hand. "What brings you to Paris?"

"Uh." Dorothy cleared her throat and glanced at the little stuffed animal again. "I'm visiting a few places my late husband and I vacationed to many years ago."

"Oh, that's so sweet!" said Karlee. She clasped a hand over her heart and smiled a sappy grin.

Karen smiled in kind understanding. "Well, welcome. I hope you have a good time. Are you coming to the dinner tonight?"

Dorothy hesitated and cleared her throat. "I-I'm not

sure yet."

"Oh, don't worry yourself, dear. You will be welcome to attend, but if you cannot, we understand."

"Karlee!" someone called across the show hall.

"Trista!" Karlee called back. She hooked her arm around Dorothy's again, and said, "Come on. Let me introduce you to my friends."

Reluctantly, Dorothy was pulled up one of the rows of cages and then quite maddeningly pounced upon by a gaggle of young girls who squealed almost as much as Karlee. They spoke amongst themselves very quickly in French and pulled out their cats for Dorothy to see and pet. She was beginning to feel her breath coming faster as the girls' excitement permeated the air.

"Ms. Fennec," said a voice behind the woman. She inhaled and turned, coming face-to-face with Jeff Martin. He was still stern, his thumbs hooked in his belt loops. "Making new friends, are we?" Something about him made the hair on the back of Dorothy's neck stand on end.

"I'm sorry we did not get to speak more at the café," Dorothy said. It had not escaped her attention that the gaggle of girls behind her had gone silent.

"I'm sorrier about Ms. Rhor's croquembouche." He seemed to attempt a smile, but it came across more as a grimace.

"Indeed," said Dorothy. "I haven't seen her here yet."

Jeff cast a casual look around the hall. "Nor have I. It's rather odd for her, considering she's the director of this region. Perhaps the loss of her… pastry… is hitting her harder than expected."

Dorothy flashed a smile, but it immediately fell. "Yes, well, I should return to my –" Dorothy turned to the girls behind her. They were all pretending to brush and pet a single cat, who was beginning to look more disgruntled by the moment.

Jeff nodded and walked away. Dorothy let out a sigh she hadn't realized she had been holding in.

"Oh, my gosh. He is so creepy!" one of the girls behind Dorothy said.

"He certainly isn't very personable," Dorothy replied. The cat they had been brushing swatted at one of the girls, and she promptly returned the cat to its cage.

"I heard his last litter weren't actually purebreds," said one of the girls.

"I heard he knows he's not going to get the regional directorship again," said another.

"I heard he killed his wife." All the girls collapsed on Karlee, shushing her and giggling. "But no, for real.

I heard his hair is a toupee made from his cat's hair. It's not real." She whispered these last words, and her friends began laughing uncontrollably.

Dorothy couldn't have been more reminded how much things had changed since she had been that age – and how much she had changed.

"I've heard rumors," Dorothy began. The girls immediately stopped laughing, their attention fully on the older woman. "Of cats disappearing."

The girls looked at each other. Then, one broke down in tears.

"What's wrong?" Dorothy asked.

"One of Jenna's cats is one that's missing," said one of the girls patting the crying girl's back.

"I can't believe I don't even remember her," Jenna sobbed through her fingers.

"What happened, sweetheart?" Dorothy knelt beside the girl and pulled a travel pack of tissues from her jacket. Dorothy had never had children of her own, but her mothering instincts were still in full swing.

Jenna took a tissue and blew her nose loudly. She sniffed a few times and wiped the tears from her cheeks, leaving a streak of blue mascara. "Well, I must have put her in the cage, because her number was on top of it. I was watching Michaela's Bengal get judged when I heard the clerk in my ring calling for number

27. My little Jonesy was number 28, so I thought I would check out the book and see who 27 was so I could find them and let them know. But…"

Jenna inhaled, trying to stifle her tears. Karlee threw her arms around the girl and hugged her. Jenna blew her nose again and continued. "But it was me. I ran back to my cage, but I didn't have any more cats. I – I couldn't remember having brought two cats. I asked Karlee, and she didn't remember either. It was so scary. She had points in the catalog, points that went back for several shows. I was scrolling through my phone, and I found pictures of a cat that fit her description playing with Jonesy. But no one knew who she was."

"And I had just said earlier that day how beautiful your Siberians always turn out," Karlee whispered.

Dorothy frowned. "You breed Siberians?" Jenna nodded. "I believe Mr. Martin is also a Siberian breeder."

All the girls stared at Dorothy wide-eyed.

"Yeah," Jenna breathed. "He is. You don't think…"

Dorothy stood and smiled. "Don't worry yourself, sweetheart," she said to Jenna. She handed her the rest of the tissue pack and pulled out several butterscotch candies she always kept in her coat pockets. "I'm sure everything will sort itself out. If you need anything, you come find me, all right?"

Jenna nodded and Dorothy handed each girl a candy before excusing herself back to her own cage area.

The show hall was becoming louder and more crowded. Vendors were beginning to set up their tables along the outer edges of the caging area. Shelves lined with decorative cat plates and boxes full of feline-themed jewelry. Even brushes, shampoos and colored powders for what, Dorothy had no idea.

She gathered up the hotel cart and headed for the door, Jeff Martin conveniently several paces ahead of her.

The hotel cart transitioned from the carpeted hallway to the tile of the main lobby. Jeff glanced over his shoulder when he heard the wheels hit the tile behind him. Dorothy glanced down at the wheels of the cart and acted as though she were adjusting her steering. Jeff pressed the button for the elevator and stepped inside. Dorothy picked up her pace and thrust a hand through the closing elevator doors.

She smiled at him. "Phew! Glad I caught you. Solomon must be starving by now," she said. Jeff continued to scowl. She pushed the cart into the elevator, forcing Jeff to shift his position. "Floor?" she asked him.

"Three," he said gruffly. Dorothy pressed the button for the third floor and felt the elevator lift off.

Jeff crossed his arms and shuffled his feet, staring determinedly at the floor. Dorothy's hands shook, and a chill ran up her spine. She cleared her throat and adjusted her cardigan. The elevator slowed and gave a soft ding as it stopped at the third floor. Dorothy shuffled out with the hotel cart and waited for Jeff to step out in front of her. He did so begrudgingly, and she followed him up the hallway. He stopped in front of one of the doors and fumbled for his room key. Dorothy walked past him, glancing briefly at the room number on the door. She left the cart in the hall and turned down the hallway toward the vending machines. She heard the soft beep and click as Jeff's door opened.

Dorothy peeked her head around the corner just as the door clicked shut. Room 315.

ᴇIGHT

SOLOMON HAD CURLED UP ON THE END OF the hotel bed. He lifted his head when Dorothy entered and yawned widely at her.

"Nice to see you too," she said with a grin.

There was a faint ringing from the suitcase she had yet to unpack. Solomon stretched, flopped onto his side, and glowered at the suitcase on the floor.

Dorothy unzipped the sides and rummaged through before pulling out a small tablet. The screen was black except for the word Destin across the top with an answer and dismiss button at the bottom. It also read *12 missed calls* below Destin's name. She swiped to accept the call, and Destin's face appeared on the screen.

"Thank God," Destin said. "We thought you had been compromised."

Dorothy blinked at him. She didn't own a tablet and wondered how it had gotten into her suitcase.

"Destin?" she asked.

"Fennec, where were you?"

Dorothy blinked again and sat on the corner of the bed. "Investigating. Isn't that what I'm supposed to be doing?"

Destin sighed, a small smile pulling at his lips. "Yes. Yes, you are. What have you found?"

"Sharon has a bracelet, but that's all I know. Karen's grandson passed away about a year ago. She carries around a stuffed animal that used to belong to him."

"Hmm." Destin grabbed his chin in thought. "Emotions projected onto a physical object could manifest an artifact."

"Well, I believe I have a lead with Jeff Martin," Dorothy said. She kicked off her shoes and watched as Solomon jumped from the bed to thoroughly investigate them with his nose.

Destin shifted in his seat. "What sort of lead?"

"I spoke with one of the girls who has been affected by this… whatever this is. She breeds the same sort of cat as Jeff, and…" Dorothy trailed off as Solomon leapt back onto the bed and pushed his way onto Dorothy's lap to look at the screen. "There's something very odd about him."

"Have you been able to plant any of the tracking or audio devices?"

"No, but I know Jeff's room number now. If you can get me a key, I might be able to get in while everyone is at the dinner Sharon and Karen mentioned."

Destin reached across his desk and Solomon batted at the screen, causing it to minimize.

"Solomon!" Dorothy scolded, and the cat jumped away. "Destin?" she asked. "Are you still there?"

"Of course, what happened?"

"The cat. I'm trying –"

"It's all right, Fennec. Now, listen carefully. You will have an envelope delivered to your room shortly. It will contain the room numbers and keys for all three targets. Get in and get out with those trackers, then report back as soon as the job is complete."

"What happens if I'm caught?" Dorothy asked.

There was a pause, and Destin replied, "Don't get caught." There was a small beep, and the program returned to its home screen. Dorothy stared at the tablet until Solomon leapt on the bed again, meowing innocently. She set the tablet on the desk and pulled out a tin of canned food.

But Solomon didn't seem to notice. He jumped from the bed and ran to the door. He sniffed at the bottom gap, then ran back to Dorothy, winding himself around her ankles. Dorothy looked at the door and noticed a shadow shifting. She set the tin down and followed the cat to the door.

Through the little peephole, Dorothy glimpsed a head full of pink hair. Karlee stepped back from the door, where she had pressed her ear to the wood. She glanced at the peephole and lifted a hand to knock. Dorothy pulled the door open before she could. Karlee startled and stepped back.

"Hello, Karlee," Dorothy said sweetly.

"H-Hi," Karlee said. She lowered her arm, which she still had raised above her head. "I asked the front desk which room you were in. Um, I wanted to invite you to dinner with me and the girls, but, uh –" She peered past Dorothy into the room beyond. "Can I ask you something?"

A bell boy appeared beside Karlee. "Ms. Fennec," he said as he handed Dorothy an envelope. Dorothy took it and Karlee watched the envelope with anticipation. The bell boy walked away, and Karlee looked back at Dorothy.

"Come inside, Karlee," Dorothy said.

The girl hesitated. After a moment, she

stepped through and jumped when Dorothy closed the door behind her. "Please don't hurt me! I won't tell anyone, I swear!" she said.

Dorothy's brow furrowed in confusion. "Karlee, what are you talking about?" She took a step toward the girl, but Karlee darted farther into the room, not daring to turn her back on the woman.

"I – I know you're the one causing the cats to disappear. I heard you talking about targets and –" She stopped when Dorothy started to laugh. "Please, don't hurt Jenna."

Dorothy set the envelope of room keys on the dresser and walked past the skittish girl to her suitcase. Karlee pressed herself against the far wall. She had trapped herself in the room and was unable to get to the front door without going past Dorothy. Solomon walked up to her, setting a paw on her leg and meowing softly. Dorothy pulled out the envelope Destin had given her at the antique shop and held it out to her.

Karlee looked from Dorothy to the envelope. Solomon meowed at her again and rubbed against her leg. She reached out a shaking hand and took the envelope. Dorothy walked to the desk and began heating up some water in the tiny coffee pot. By the time the pink-haired girl had finished sifting through the papers, Dorothy had brewed two cups of Earl Grey. She handed one to the girl and gestured toward the small recliner in the corner. Karlee sat with a loud thud, and Solomon immediately jumped into her lap.

"You're – you're a spy?" Karlee whispered.

Dorothy smirked. "Something like that."

"So, who do you think it is?"

"I'm not sure." Dorothy blew across the top of her tea and took a sip. Karlee mimicked her and stroked the cat that had made himself comfortable across her lap.

"Well, I totally think it's Jeff Martin," said Karlee, her bubbly attitude returning. "I mean, he's been acting so weird lately."

"That is true," said Dorothy. "But I haven't ruled out Karen yet either."

"Karen?" Karlee asked surprised. "Oh, no. No, no. Not her. Karen's like really old." Dorothy raised an eyebrow and Karlee hesitated. Dorothy winked at her, and Karlee gave a stifled laugh. "But she couldn't do anything like this. Her grandson died, like, a year ago, and she was so upset. I don't think Karen is the kind of person who would steal cats and make people lose their memories."

Dorothy took a sip of her tea again. It wasn't very good tea. She sat in silence for several minutes, then sighed.

"Karlee, do you think you and your friends could help me?" she asked.

Karlee sat up a little straighter. "Oh, of course.

Anything!"

Dorothy rose and picked up the envelope the bell boy had given her. "This could be very dangerous. Are you sure?"

Karlee set her cup on the edge of the dresser and stood. She stuck out her chin, her arms straight at her sides. "Definitely."

Karlee had gathered her gaggle of girlfriends to her hotel room in no time flat. They sat scattered around Karlee's room, sitting cross-legged on the floor, sprawled across the bed, and even perched on top of the dresser. Her cats, two odd-eyed Khao Manees, were preoccupied with playing fetch with Michaela. Dorothy wondered if she would be able to get the girls to focus between the fetching felines and the stuffed crust pizza Jenna had ordered.

"Oh, my gosh! It's so cute!" Brittany exclaimed as she picked up a small cat statue next to her on the dresser. "Is this one from Scott too?"

Karlee nodded and smiled. "He's still studying in Cairo, so I haven't been able to talk to him for a few weeks."

"They look like those little Egyptian jars," said Jenna

studying the collection Karlee had amassed over the last several shows.

"Canopic," Dorothy said, and the girls turned to look at her. "They are called canopic jars. They held the preserved organs of the deceased. The Egyptians believed extracting and preserving specific organs was necessary for the person's soul to transcend and continue in the afterlife."

"Gross," Michaela whispered.

"I think it's cool." Jenna took the jar from Brittany and examined it.

"Okay, ladies. This is very important, so listen up." Karlee clapped her hands, and her friends went silent.

Dorothy cleared her throat and sat a little straighter. "The disappearance of these cats is, of course, quite troublesome. It is unknown by what means our perpetrator may be doing this, and if their targets may eventually go beyond cats." The girls stared at Dorothy, and the woman was quite sure they were all holding their breath. She continued, pulling the small bags of GPS trackers and audio recorders from the pocket of her cardigan. "As such, it is important that our targets start getting tracked."

"Tracked?" Michaela asked. "Like spied on?"

"In a sense, yes. If you young ladies are amicable to the idea, I need a tracker and audio recorder placed in each room." Dorothy held up the two bags of GPS trackers and audio dots. There is little time for me to do all three on my own. Are you willing to help me?"

All the girls nodded excitedly and grinned with anticipation.

"You need to place these so they will be on our targets during the show tomorrow. We need to track their movements as well as any conversations they might have. Can you guarantee that?"

Again, the girls nodded. Dorothy nodded as well and began passing out the little dots. "We have three targets. We'll break into teams of two. Does anyone know when the dinner is tonight?"

"It starts at seven at the restaurant attached to the hotel," said Jenna.

"Then that is when we begin," the old woman said.

"Can we call it Operation Feline?" asked Trista eagerly.

"Ooh, what about Operation Catwoman?" said Michaela.

"Girls!" Karlee quickly redirected her friends' attention, and they fell silent. Dorothy suppressed a smile, her admiration for Karlee growing by the minute. "It doesn't matter what it's called. This is a real situation here. It's not a game. Maybe we can get Jenna's cat back – and don't forget, our memories.

None of us remember anything about these cats. If whatever is causing this can be used for more than just cats, what happens if it makes us forget that we're friends?"

Silence. The girls looked at each other and fidgeted uncomfortably.

"We have one hour," said Dorothy. "Let's move."

NINE

KARLEE AND DOROTHY STOOD BY THE vending machines on the third floor. Karlee's phone flashed again as Brittany and Jenna, and Trista and Michaela joined their group call.

"B and J on standby," Brittany whispered.

"M and T on standby," Trista whispered.

"K and D on standby. Wait for your targets to move out, then we'll move in. Over," said Karlee.

"You don't have to say 'over,' Karlee," said Trista.

"Oh, right. *Pardon.*" Karlee blushed and giggled.

Dorothy stared into the vending machine and fingered the trackers in her pocket. Her heart raced. She hoped she could trust these girls. She had barely met Karlee and her friends two hours ago. But she supposed being a spy meant following one's instincts. She only hoped her instincts were right. The years brought wisdom, but they also brought things like failing memory as well.

"Target two is leaving. Repeat, target two is leaving!" came Trista's voice over the phone.

"Ssh!" said Karlee, "Don't give yourself away!"

"Sorry," Trista whispered. "She's getting in the elevator now… the doors are closing… aaand… we're going in."

Karlee looked at Dorothy and smiled. Dorothy nodded back, her heart racing even more. Karen Augusta was about to be checked off the list.

"Target one is leaving," came Brittany's voice, more hushed and calm than Trista's had been. "We're a go."

Dorothy could only imagine how silly the girls looked, possibly doing somersaults across the halls and up to the doors. She sighed, casting the thought from her mind. Destin had never mentioned the security cameras. She hoped he had thought to take care of that as well.

A door opened from somewhere in the hall. Karlee peeked her head around the corner, then whipped back into the small room. She gave Dorothy a thumbs up before peering around the corner again. She motioned for Dorothy to move out.

The hall was deserted, and Dorothy heard the elevator doors close around the corner. She inserted the key card into the lock of Room 315. The little light turned green and clicked loudly. Carefully, Dorothy opened the door.

The room was a mirror opposite of her own. In the corner beside the desk was a small show cage, where a fluffy white cat lay inside. It lifted its head, blinked at Dorothy, and went back to sleep.

The desk and bed were scattered with paperwork. Dorothy glanced over the papers. Someone had marked them with a red pen and had written in the margins.

Lowest earning Persian one of the notes read. Late entry for Baton Rouge show said another. There were at least twelve names, all with varying sized stacks of paper and red-penned notes.

Dorothy pulled out her phone and snapped several pictures before returning to her search of the room. She opened the door to the closet. Inside, several button-downs hung loosely on their hangers accompanied by slacks and a belt. She couldn't be sure which one Jeff would wear tomorrow versus Sunday. She saw a pair of brown dress shoes sitting perfectly one beside the other on the floor under the clothes. It would seem like an easy place to put a GPS tracker, but there was too much risk of the tracker being crushed or even discovered if it rubbed on Jeff's foot too much.

She closed the closet door again and began pacing the room. Nothing stood out to her. There was movement in the hallway, and Dorothy saw a shadow pass by the door.

"Mr. Martin!" she heard Karlee call. Dorothy froze. "Hey, uh, I was wondering if I could talk to you for a minute."

Dorothy threw the closet door open again and darted inside. She heard the click of the lock and immediately kicked herself. How stupid of her. The shower would have been a better place, or anywhere in the bathroom. The bathroom…

"See, I–I was thinking about maybe breeding a Siberian, ya know. Instead of an Egyptian Mau. I mean, I know Scott wants a Mau, but the Siberians are so –"

Dorothy rushed from the closet as Karlee continued to ramble on. She glanced around the dark room, looking for a watch. Her eyes set on an engraved name tag. It was Jeff's Regional Director tag. She quickly flipped it over and attached the tiny dots of the GPS tracker and the audio recorder to the bottom corners.

"I'm sorry, Karlee can we –"

Dorothy heard a loud *CRASH* in the hallway. She darted to the door and glanced out the peephole. Both Jeff and Karlee peered at the remnants of a decorative vase that had stood across from the room, and a phone that had shattered into several pieces. The man's back was to her. She squeezed out of the door that cracked open from Jeff's return and ran several paces up the hallway before turning around and heading back toward Karlee and Jeff.

"Karlee?" she asked, slightly out of breath. Both Jeff and Karlee looked up. Jeff scowled at the woman, and Dorothy saw Karlee breathe a sigh of relief. "Are you all right?"

"She's fine, Ms. Fennec. Just a slip of the hand. Her phone fell," said Jeff as he straightened himself to stand taller.

Dorothy looked at Karlee and the girl nodded. "It's okay. I've got insurance on it. Um, I'm sorry Mr. Martin. I'll catch up with you later."

Jeff nodded and headed into his room. Karlee bent to pick up the pieces of her shattered phone among the shards of vase, tears beginning to fall down her face. Dorothy squeezed Karlee's shoulder.

"You were marvelous, Karlee! Thank you," she whispered.

"No, it's not that," Karlee breathed.

"Don't worry about the vase. It wasn't expensive, believe me. And I can replace your phone, sweetheart. I'm so sorry. That was incredibly brave of you."

"No, it's –" Karlee held out her hand to Dorothy. Four out of five nails were painted in a bright, electric blue with tiny jewels glued on in the shape of a paw print. Her last fingernail was bare, save for a few pieces of dried glue. "I know it's stupid, but I just had these done yesterday."

Dorothy couldn't help but laugh. She helped Karlee gather the pieces of her phone, and they headed back to the girl's room.

The four other girls were congregated outside her door, looks of relief spreading across their faces when they saw Dorothy and Karlee.

"Oh. Mon. Dieu! We thought you guys died or something!" said Michaela and she flung her arms around Karlee.

"Your call dropped and we all panicked," said Brittany.

"Were you able to place your trackers?" Dorothy asked. All four girls nodded.

"And we found something weird in Sharon's room," Jenna whispered.

Dorothy lifted an eyebrow at the girl, then jerked her head toward Karlee's hotel room door. They filed in and the girls immediately spread out into their previous places about the room. Karlee reached into her mini-fridge and pulled out a six-pack of wine coolers. She passed one to each of her friends, then offered one to Dorothy. The woman declined. It was difficult for her to imagine these girls were old enough to drink. They barely felt old enough to be out of school. But then everyone Dorothy met seemed to be getting younger and younger.

"What did you find?" Dorothy finally asked after the girls had taken several long drinks from the bottles.

Brittany wiped a dribble from her chin. "There was a really big, old cookbook lying on the bed. It was opened to something…" She trailed off, thinking. "What did you say it was?" she asked Jenna.

"It was like a tower of little balls. Croaky something."

"Croquembouche?" Dorothy asked.

"That's it!" said Jenna. "What's a croqu-ee-bush?"

"It is a tower of soft pastries held together by a light caramel drizzle," Dorothy replied.

"You are like, tres smart," said Trista, taking another sip of her wine cooler.

"But what's a cork-an-brush have to do with cats?" Karlee asked.

"*Oh, mon DIEU!*" Jenna practically screamed. "She's cooking our cats!" The girl immediately burst into tears. Trista caught her wine cooler bottle before it fell on the floor.

Dorothy tried to console the girl. "I don't think that's

the case, Jenna."

"But what else is it then?" Jenna croaked through her fingers.

"I believe I have an explanation." Jenna went silent and they all stared at Dorothy again. "When I first met Sharon, it was at a small café down the street. She had ordered a croquembouche to be delivered to the show hall tomorrow as a treat for everyone. But it fell out of its box onto the floor. She was quite upset. I imagine she was looking up a recipe to see if she could make one herself."

"But where would she make it at? She doesn't have a kitchen in her hotel room," said Michaela.

"Maybe she was gonna ask if she could use the hotel kitchen? Or someone else at the hotel?" Brittany shrugged her shoulders.

"Doesn't Sharon live in Paris?" Karlee asked. "What's she doing staying at the hotel if she lives here?"

No one had an explanation.

Shortly thereafter, the girls became quite giggly again. Dorothy excused herself and headed up the hall to her own room. She could hear Solomon meowing for her as soon as she rounded the corner. The cat had probably heard everything that had occurred during the incident with Jeff and Karlee. She opened the door, and Solomon continued his incessant meowing in a seemingly reprimanding tone.

"Yes, Mother," Dorothy said to the cat, who followed her across the room. He finally quieted himself into a constant purr and settled at the foot of the bed.

Dorothy kicked off her shoes again and powered on the tablet. The home screen seemed rather normal. It contained several familiar icons for social media sites and a few web browsers. One icon caught her eye, however. It was a simple, silver square with the words Fox's Den beneath it. Dorothy tapped the icon and saw the familiar video panel she had used to speak to Destin earlier. But this time, it was blank. She tapped a green button at the bottom that read *Call Fox Den*.

After several moments of silence, Destin's face appeared on the screen again.

"Ms. Fennec," he greeted her. "Is everything all right?"

"Of course," said Dorothy, a bit confused. "You asked me to call you."

"Yes, I did," said Destin. He appeared flustered. "I wasn't expecting you to contact me so soon."

Dorothy furrowed her brow. "Soon? I was going to apologize for taking so long."

Destin smiled and ran a hand over his hair. "You're more like your father than you know, Ms. Fennec.

Have the trackers been placed then?"

"Yes." Dorothy nodded. "I found several papers in Mr. Martin's room, though, that I would like to send to you." She held up her phone for Destin to see. The man directed her on connecting her cell phone to the tablet and sending the photos of the red-marked papers. The process took several minutes, but Dorothy was not foreign to technology. She had used it quite frequently while working at the museum.

"Are any of these names familiar?" she asked.

Destin sighed. "Unfortunately, they are. Except for one." Dorothy was silent, waiting for Destin to continue. "This is a list of every victim thus far, save for one."

"Who?" Dorothy pressed, and she felt her heart beat a little faster.

"Sharon Rhors."

TEN

DOROTHY WALKED UP THE NOW-BUSTLING
Parisian street back to the hotel. A bakery box was
tucked securely under one arm, and Solomon's leash
in her other hand. She entered the hotel and brushed
her windswept hair back into place. Several people
in the lobby smiled when they saw Solomon, and the
little cat trotted up to them for pets. A pair of the cat
show breeders walked by. They rolled their eyes and
scoffed at Solomon.

"Disgusting," one mumbled to the other.

"I can't believe she let her cat on that nasty floor,"
said the other. They walked away, pushing their large
Maine Coons inside cramped cages on a hotel cart
toward the show hall.

Dorothy ignored them. She shifted the box under her
arm and led Solomon away from his many admirers

toward the show hall.

The vendors and other cat breeders smiled their greetings at Solomon when Dorothy entered the show hall. It took her several minutes to make it to her benching area. Everyone seemed to marvel at the little black cat on his leash and harness, and Solomon was all too keen to make friends with everyone. She set the box on her chair and hoisted Solomon into his cage. Karlee turned from grooming her cat and smiled at Dorothy and Solomon. She cooed over the little cat and offered him bits of a tuna treat, which he quickly scarfed down.

"How's Jenna?" Dorothy asked. "I hope she wasn't too upset after I left."

"She's all right," Karlee replied, glancing across the sea of cages toward her friend. "Michaela was able to calm her down. Jenna gets worked up over weird stuff like that."

Dorothy nodded and shifted the box again. "Would you like to see something?"

Karlee's eyes sparkled with curiosity. Very carefully, Dorothy undid the bottom of the pastry box. She lifted it up and revealed a large, golden croquembouche.

"This is a croquembouche," she said.

"Wow," Karlee breathed. She played with the pendant around her neck and reached out a hand toward one of the little pillow-like pastries.

"Now, hold on." Dorothy laughed at her and pulled the tower of pastries away. "This is for Sharon. Come with me."

This time, Dorothy led Karlee through the show hall. Heads turned as she made her way past the judging rings and then toward Sharon's cat cage. The woman didn't notice at first. It wasn't until Dorothy and Karlee had stopped behind her that the woman looked up. She gasped, her hand clapping over her mouth. Her eyes looked like they were ready to pop out of her head.

"A croquembouche," she breathed. Dorothy smiled and held the stand out for Sharon to take. "For me? Dorothy, I –"

Dorothy shook her head. "Please, it was my pleasure."

Sharon took the stand with trembling hands and placed the golden dessert on an empty table beside her cage. Several breeders had gathered and were ooh-ing over the gift.

"I – I was going to go home and make one, but I wouldn't have had time. It's why I'm at the hotel. Parisian traffic is the worst. Oh, Dorothy." Sharon kissed Dorothy on each cheek three times and squeezed both of her hands in delight.

"Croquembouche for everyone!" she called in French to the crowd that had gathered. Dorothy smiled as she watched Sharon offer the small dough balls to the people closest to her. She backed away quietly and headed back to her benching area.

"That was really nice of you," said Karlee from behind her. "Why'd you do that when she's one of our suspects?" Her mouth was now full of one of the little pastry balls.

Dorothy raised an eyebrow at the girl. "Our suspects?" Karlee blushed and wiped crumbs from the corner of her mouth. "Because it hurts no one to be a kind person, regardless of the other person's character."

"Oh," Karlee said quietly.

"And," Dorothy continued, "there is an additional tracker under the croquembouche stand. A good croquembouche should never go to waste."

There was the screech of a microphone. Dorothy and Karlee looked up to see a thin blonde woman standing in the center judging ring and holding one of the microphones. She spoke in French very quickly, and Dorothy looked to Karlee for help.

"All of the directors who are here are holding a special meeting," she said. "They're asking everyone to come." Dorothy followed Karlee to the ring. Jeff

Martin stood beside three other women, including the blonde woman who had just spoken over the microphone. He frowned at the gathering crowd until his gaze landed on Dorothy. They locked eyes for a moment until he finally looked away. He shoved his thumbs in his belt loops and puffed out his chest. Dorothy suppressed a smirk. Jeff's director name tag was displayed prominently on his shirt pocket.

"Merci à tous d'être venus," said the blonde woman. *"Nous allons garder ce bref."*

Brittany, Jenna, Michaela, and Trista joined Karlee and Dorothy as the blonde woman continued in French.

"She's talking about the disappearance of the cats," Karlee whispered to Dorothy. "She says that if you see anything suspicious to inform one of the regional managers here at the show. They don't want to cause a panic."

Michaela put an arm around Jenna and gave her a reassuring squeeze.

"C'est tout ce que nous avons pour vous, alors s'il vous plaît amusez-vous et profitez du spectacle!"

The crowd clapped politely and dispersed.

"So, what's the plan?" Brittany whispered to Dorothy.

"Plan?" the woman asked.

"Yeah," said Trista. "What do you need us to do?"

Dorothy glanced over her shoulder. Jeff was watching them closely. "I want you to keep your eyes out for anything odd. Tell me immediately if you see or hear anything. But right this moment, I want you to laugh like I said something funny, and then go back to your areas. Do not turn and look at Mr. Martin."

The girls squealed with a very believable laughter. Trista even snorted, which did make the girls begin to laugh even harder. They hugged Dorothy and hurried back to their benching areas. The microphones chirped again as the clerks began to announce which cats were to go to which ring.

"That's you!" said Karlee, who had stayed by Dorothy's side.

"What?" Dorothy asked.

Karlee giggled. "Number 452. Solomon. He's up in ring three."

"Gracious, I nearly forgot!" Dorothy turned on her heel and immediately felt something crack in her hip. She limped as quickly as she could back toward Solomon and his cage.

"Calm down. You've got a minute or two," said Karlee. She seemed to float effortlessly beside the old woman, her bright pink hair swaying in stride. When Dorothy didn't respond, Karlee ducked in front of her.

Dorothy halted, and Karlee set her hands on Dorothy's elbows. She smiled sweetly at her and took a deep breath, prompting Dorothy to do the same. "He'll pick up on your energy. Relax, Madame Fennec. We've got you covered." The girl hooked her arm through Dorothy's as she had the previous day. She led her back to Solomon and Karlee's Khao Manees.

"Are you ready to be a fancy show kitty, Solomon?" Karlee cooed at the cat. Solomon put his paws on the front of the cage and waited for the girl to take him out. Karlee set him on her grooming table and ran a brush through his coat, talking softly and gently as she did. She cleaned his ears and trimmed his nails, and made sure to give the cat plenty of treats as she did so. Then, she placed Solomon in Dorothy's arms. She winked at Dorothy and bustled off with an odd-eyed cat slung over her shoulder.

Dorothy watched her go and felt her heart lighten. She hadn't needed to lecture Karlee. Kindness came naturally to her. She scratched Solomon's ears absentmindedly, and the cat began to purr. "Now, you behave yourself, young man," she whispered to the cat. "Remember, we have to blend in. No flipping out like a little ninja cat now, hear me?"

Solomon answered her with a single meow and sat down, his paws placed perfectly centered. Dorothy rolled her eyes and scooped the cat up, heading for the show ring.

She placed Solomon in the cage marked with his number. She struggled with the little wire door until Solomon was batting at her hand through the cage.

"*Comme ci*," said a woman beside Dorothy, and she reached over, showing Dorothy how to secure the cage.

"Merci," said Dorothy, heading out of the ring. She stood at the back of the group that had gathered there, glancing up and down the row of judging rings. Karen Augusta stood behind her table, a giant Savannah sprawled out before her. She hoped the girls had been able to find something to attach her GPS tracker and audio device to.

She looked at the stuffed little cat beside her podium. Could something so innocent truly be the culprit in all this? Her thoughts drifted to Frank again, and how there was a part of her heart that would forever be empty. She knew she could never fill that void, but Solomon had helped ease her pain. Could it be so simple?

She felt someone nudge her arm. The woman who had helped her close the cage door pointed. The judge had approached Solomon. He placed his paws on the door, waiting to be let out. The judge opened the wire cage and gathered the cat into her arms. Dorothy saw him snuggle into her neck.

"He's good," the woman beside her said in a heavy French accent. "Knows how to win the judges, *oui?*"

Solomon stood on the podium and stared out at the crowd. He gave a small meow, then stretched himself up onto the scratching pole beside the table. The crowd awed over him and watched as he ran in circles after a toy the judge had brought out for him. When he caught the toy, he flopped on his side and licked it, before turning his green, doe eyes up to the judge. She laughed, scooped Solomon into her arms and returned him to his cage.

"I'm not exactly sure that's blending in," Dorothy mumbled to herself.

The day passed by in a blur. Dorothy shuffled Solomon to and from the judging rings and spent the rest of her time walking the aisles and speaking with the breeders. Sharon's croquembouche had been devoured in a matter of minutes. Every time the woman saw Dorothy, she kissed her on the cheek and thanked her for her act of kindness.

Karen Augusta seemed more serious, even stern, now that she was behind the judging table. Dorothy watched as she scrutinized each cat before placing it back in its cage without a word. The only time she seemed excited was when she placed her top ten cats in each category.

Dorothy did her best to avoid Jeff Martin. The man loomed ominously in the background wherever she went. He paced back and forth, always a few feet from Dorothy. The feeling in the pit of her stomach told her he was following her. It was in her last show ring of the day her suspicions were confirmed.

Dorothy stood at the back of the crowd once more. She watched as Solomon gave another spectacularly adorable performance, then cast about for Sharon. Dorothy was determined to keep an eye on her.

"Are you enjoying your time in Paris, Ms. Fennec?"

Dorothy jumped at the sound of the voice. She turned to see Jeff staring down at her, his eyes narrowed and his thumbs still hooked in his belt loops.

"Yes. Yes, I am," she replied, turning back to watch a little gray tabby cat scale the entire scratching pole.

"That was quite the act with the croquembouche. A masterful one, I might add."

Dorothy whipped around again. "And what is that supposed to mean, Mr. Martin? Can no one do a good deed for the sake of what's right anymore?"

"Not if that deed is for the sake of something more ill-advised." He grunted at her. Dorothy narrowed her own eyes, staring the man down.

"I don't know what you're talking about," Dorothy snapped. Her head felt foggy for a moment. She blinked as a small bout of dizziness washed over her, but she pushed the feeling away.

"No?" Mr. Martin asked. "Then why are you here, Ms. Fennec? You have no cat, and yet I have seen you here not only today but yesterday as well. You were conveniently meeting Ms. Rhors at the café when I walked in. I am not blind, and I will not let anything happen to anyone within this organization, human or otherwise."

Dorothy blinked, trying to find the right words. Why was she here? If she had no cat to show, what cover could she possibly use to disguise her true mission?

A murmur from the crowd caught Dorothy's attention. She turned. Several people were flipping through their show catalogs pointing at an empty cage.

"Ms. Fennec!" Karlee ran up behind Jeff. She took a step back as the man glowered down at her. She broke from his gaze and pushed her way past him.

"What is it?" Dorothy asked.

Karlee's gaggle of friends joined her, each carrying a show catalog.

"It's – it's your cat, ma'am," said Jenna, and tears brimmed her eyes.

"My cat?" said Dorothy. "But I don't have –"
She looked up, the number above the empty cage
displayed prominently: 452.

&LEVEN

KARLEE AND HER FRIENDS FOLLOWED Dorothy back to her benching area. A set of purple show curtains with emerald trim and a matching pillow with a large 'S' embroidered across the top were not only covered in black cat hair, but Dorothy's purse and other personal items were strewn about the area. The curtains and pillow weren't ghastly, but they were more extravagant than Dorothy would have ever purchased. She remembered her ride on the plane and finding them on one of the seats. From Miss Kitty, the note had said.

Dorothy pulled out her phone and began flipping through her pictures. There were a few from the plane, mostly of pristine little landscapes below the cloud lines, but there he was. A little black cat with bright green eyes. He was looking out the window, sitting on the purple pillow. There were pictures of him at Dorothy's old apartment. In the background of one, she could see a picture she had taken with Frank many years ago. They had been visiting the monasteries of Tibet. Except in this picture, a tiny black kitten was held between them.

Dorothy sat in her chair beside the show cage, Karlee and her friends staring at her in silence. There was no denying she had owned a cat. She looked up from her phone and stared across the hall. Through the sea of faces that looked quickly away from her, she saw Sharon Rhors. The woman cuddled an Egyptian Mau and looked incredibly nervous. Was Sharon still the target, or had the disappearance of Dorothy's cat cleared that target? She had been talking to Jeff when the incident had occurred. He had been the one to mention she did not have a cat. Either this was how he made the cats disappear, or it completely cleared him of being involved. Dorothy wasn't sure. She was confused and alert and numb.

She had been lightheaded moments before Karlee had approached her. It must have been the effects of the artifact. At least she remembered that much. But not remembering a cat who had been part of her life for years was more than troubling.

Dorothy set the phone next to her and held her head

in her hands.

"Oh, he's so adorable!" said Karlee. Jenna came up behind the woman and rubbed her back. "Oh, I wish I could have him."

Dorothy paused a moment and blinked at the pink-haired girl. "What did you say, Karlee?"

The girl stood straight and played with the pendant around her neck. "I said I wish I could have him, but, I say that about almost all the cats I see."

The woman reached out a hand and looked closer at the girl's necklace. It was heavy and made from clay with poured glass and jewels. Dorothy heard a faint rattling sound when it moved. It was small, but most certainly not a knock-off.

"Karlee, where did you say you got this?"

Karlee pressed her hand to the pendant. "Scott. My-My fiancé. He's in Egypt right now –"

"May I see your pendant, please?" Dorothy held out a hand, making sure to keep a calm demeanor so as not to frighten Karlee away. Her friends had already taken a few tentative steps back, their eyes flitting back and forth between the young hipster girl and the old woman.

Karlee fell silent. Her bottom lip began to tremble as she pulled the chain over her head. Dorothy laid the necklace on the table in front of her gingerly and took several pictures. She handed it back to Karlee, then pulled up her phone's contact list.

It rang several times until a familiar voice answered. "Thank you for calling Richard's Anecdotes. This is Aaron. How many I help you today?"

"Aaron, it's Ms. Cl–Dorothy," she said quietly.

"Ms. Claes! It is good to hear from you. How is Paris?" Aaron asked politely.

"It's interesting. Uh, Aaron, I have a favor to ask you. If you need to close the shop to do so, you have my permission."

"Yes, ma'am," Aaron replied, his voice more serious now.

"I am going to send you some pictures of a pendant. It's Egyptian in nature. Aaron, I need you to do as much research as you can on any of the symbology present on this pendant and then call me immediately. See if there is any connection to the Egyptian Goddess Bast."

"The cat goddess, ma'am?" Aaron asked.

"Yes. See if that pulls up any results for you," the woman said.

"Would this have anything to do with the cat bed in the front window, ma'am? I've been trying to figure out why it is there for the last several minutes."

Dorothy cleared her throat. "Something like that.

Please be quick. If necessary, you may use my name at the Boston Museum with the current curator there."

"Yes, ma'am. Enjoy your trip." Aaron hung up the phone, and Dorothy forwarded the pictures to his cell phone number.

When she turned back to address the group of girls around her, she saw Jeff Martin looming behind them.

"Girls, will you excuse us a moment?" Dorothy asked. Karlee and her friends headed off into the crowd. They glanced over their shoulders, their faces somber as they went.

Dorothy stood and acknowledged the large man before her.

"Mr. Martin," she said.

"Ms. Fennec, I wish to apologize for suspecting you in this matter. Whatever it is," he said. He unhooked his thumbs from his belt loops and held out a hand to Dorothy.

The woman hesitated, then shook it. "Apology accepted, though, in the future, you'll find you attract more flies with honey than vinegar."

Jeff flashed a genuine smile for the first time and chuckled. "My wife used to say the same thing to me. I suppose old habits are hard to break."

"Jeff, can you come to ring four please?" someone called over the intercom.

"Don't stop the show," Dorothy said, touching his shoulder before the man could walk away. "We'll never find out who's doing this if we end the show. And it will only incite panic."

Jeff stared back at Dorothy, his face difficult to read. He sighed. "We're nearly done for the day. I will speak with the other directors and the show manager." He walked toward the show rings, leaving Dorothy a bit breathless and confused.

She sat in the chair again and began scrolling through her photos. There was a recent one of the cat sitting across from her at the café she and Frank used to visit when they lived in Paris. Somehow, the cat reminded her of her late husband. Outgoing, friendly. She smiled when she saw a picture of the cat eating a soufflé at the café, his face covered in egg and ham. Like Frank, the cat appeared well-traveled and clearly loved food. There was a longing in her heart, and she wondered if this cat had helped heal some of her pain when Frank had died. Was her sudden emptiness from losing Frank, or the cat she didn't know?

The microphone screeched, and she heard Jeff's voice. "Can we have everyone gather for a quick meeting please?" he said.

Dorothy rose and headed for the judging ring. Her phone buzzed in her hand. It was Aaron. She sent the call to voicemail. The boy would need to wait a moment. She settled in a chair at the back of the gathering. Karlee, Jenna, Michaela, Trista, and Brittany gathered around her. Karlee wrapped her arms around the woman's neck and hugged her. Dorothy's phone buzzed again. She swiped at the screen, sending Aaron's call to voicemail again.

"Thank you, everyone. Please, settle down. We'll make this short," said Jeff. "I'm sure by now, there is no hiding what has been happening. We all know. And we are all worried. But that is no reason to stop our shows! We have all put too much work into our cats for them not to show off their best. I can assure you that the matter is being looked into, and you will all be updated as soon as we find anything."

"What about our cats that have gone missing already? What's happened to them?" a woman asked in French, and one of the directors translated for Jeff.

"I don't have any information yet. I'm sorry. Believe me, our missing cats have not been forgotten! We are cooperating with all the proper authorities on the matter. We will find them, and we will get to the bottom of this, rest assured."

Dorothy's phone buzzed again. This time, it was a voicemail, followed by a series of pictures sent via text message.

"If you wish to leave, we won't stop you. But we would hope that everyone would stay and show that we will not back down in the face of uncertainty. We will move forward, and we will prevail over whatever this is." Jeff handed the microphone back to one of the other directors. He looked at Dorothy briefly before stepping to the side.

Dorothy finally picked up her phone as someone else began speaking into the microphone in French. There were several pictures of a computer screen. Most of the pictures depicted an Egyptian device known as a sistrum. There was also a strange hieroglyph Dorothy had never seen before: a cat-headed archer. She flipped to her voicemails and lifted the phone to her ear.

"Ma'am, you said to get back to you as quickly as I could. I-I closed the shop and called your friend at the museum. Ma'am, everything is pointing to something called Bast's Army. The priests of Bubastis – er, that is the Egyptian city dedicated to Bast, ma'am – uh, they would perform a ritual with a special device when the cats who guarded their temples became ill and elderly. The ritual was said to trap the souls of the cats in a state where they could one day be called upon by Bast as an army for a sort of Armageddon day. The symbol on this amulet is a sistrum, which is often associated with Bast. It's a sort of Egyptian maraca, ma'am. And the hieroglyph at the bottom is a representation of Bast's army. It's a very unique piece, ma'am. I hope I may see it when you return. I do hope this was helpful. I have reopened the shop, but if you need me, please give me a call, ma'am. Good day!"

Dorothy lowered the phone from her ear. Most of the crowd had dispersed, save for Karlee and her friends. They stared at Dorothy, as though waiting for an answer. They looked scared and nervous, and the woman couldn't blame them. She held out her hand to Karlee.

"Is it all right if I keep your necklace for now, Karlee?" she asked.

Reluctantly, Karlee placed her pendant in Dorothy's outstretched hand. "Is-Is this my fault, Ms. Dorothy? Did-Did I do something?" She sniffed and a single tear ran down her cheek. Dorothy held her arms open for the girl, and Karlee hugged her, followed closely by her friends. Dorothy shifted her weight so as not to be knocked over and felt her knees crack.

"No, sweetheart. It's not you or your fault. But I think your lovely gift from Scott might have something to do with this. I promise I will fix this."

TWELVE

THE ELEVATOR GAVE A SLIGHT JOLT, AND THE little bell dinged as the door slid open to the third floor. Dorothy stepped out and headed for her room. The empty feeling in her chest hadn't disappeared as she had hoped it would with time. The hotel room was eerily quiet as she stepped inside. A set of food and water dishes sat in the corner, and Dorothy saw a small stack of cat food cans on the edge of the dresser. She jumped and gave a small shriek when she stepped on something soft and furry. It was a toy mouse. With her heart now beating wildly in her chest, she kicked off her shoes and sat on the corner of the bed. She pulled out the tablet and logged into the Fox Den portal.

As she waited, she pulled a tube of pain-relieving cream from her purse and rubbed it into her knees. It was several minutes before Destin finally answered.

"Hello, Fennec! Any word on the artifact?" he asked. Dorothy held up the pendant for Destin to see, and his eyes widened. "You acquired the artifact? How?"

"It was in plain sight the entire time. Karlee's rather upset about the entire ordeal, though. She had no idea. I had Aaron do a bit of research for me, and I believe I understand what's going on. At least a little."

"Have the cats been discovered then? Have they been returned?"

Dorothy shook her head. "No, I haven't made it that far yet. I was hoping you or your organization would be able to help in that endeavor. It seems to be more of your department anyway."

Dorothy pulled up Aaron's message on her phone and played it for Destin. He smoothed his hair and nodded as he listened. When the message had finished, he sat in silence for several minutes tapping his chin and again smoothing his hair. "So, we have discovered the artifact, and we likely know what it does. But we have yet to find where the cats have disappeared to."

"In Egyptian mythology, the deceased's soul, or Ka, would descend to the underworld and take a boat across the river before having to pass through twelve trials, or gates. But this is different. It's as if the cats' souls have been trapped in a place between the living world and the underworld, waiting to return for whatever deed they were preserved for," said Dorothy.

There was a knock on Dorothy's door. "One moment, Destin," she said, rising from the bed and leaving the tablet on her pillow. Dorothy peered through the peephole and was once again greeted by a shock of bright pink hair. She opened the door, and Karlee's bloodshot eyes greeted her.

"I'm sorry to bother you, Ms. Fennec," she said. Her voice was weak and had lost every ounce of its usual brightness. "I found this in my room, and… and I thought maybe it would help you." From behind her back, the girl produced one of the familiar canopic jars. This one was not a purebred. It was black with bright green eyes. "I'm so sorry about all this. I didn't mean to hurt anyone. I–I feel horrible! *Je ne voulais pas que cela arrive.*"

She broke down in sobs, holding her tear-streaked face in her hands and sending the canopic jar plummeting to the floor. Dorothy reached out a hand and caught the Egyptian jar, breathing a sigh of relief.

"Come inside, sweetheart. I'll make you a cup of tea," she said. She ushered Karlee to the armchair beside the dresser, then turned her attention back to the tablet. Destin waited patiently as he flipped through a stack of paperwork. Dorothy picked up the tablet and carried it with her toward the little coffee pot on the desk.

"My apologies for the interruption, Destin," she said, and the man quickly turned his attention away from his paperwork. "I think we've had a breakthrough." She held up the jar for the man to see.

"What is it?" he asked, narrowing his eyes as if to see better.

"My cat. At least, I think it is."

"Solomon?" Destin cried.

"Is that the cat's name? It does sound like a name Frank and I would have come up with."

"You don't remember?"

Dorothy shook her head. "No. It's just as the reports say. And Aaron has no memory of him, either, even though he was still in Massachusetts." Dorothy narrowed her own eyes at the screen. "How have you not been affected?"

"Our headquarters are protected from the effects given off by any active artifacts. We cannot 'snag and tag,' as Red says, if we are under the influence of the artifacts we are hunting."

"You didn't think to protect me in any way while I was researching this mission?" Dorothy snapped. "And who is Red?"

"You are not yet an official member, Ms. Fennec." Destin raised an eyebrow at Dorothy, and she suppressed an eye roll that would have rivaled any of her nieces' or nephews'. Instead, she started the coffee pot to brew hot water for tea and turned her attention back to the pink-haired girl who sat clutching her knees to her chest in the armchair.

"I want you to speak with someone, Destin. She's the young lady who had the artifact. I believe she may have some useful information."

Dorothy heard Destin begin to protest but ignored him. She handed Karlee a box of tissues and the tablet. The girl's confused face matched Destin's. She wiped her eyes and blew her nose, then lifted the tablet to eye level.

"Hi," she said quietly.

"Hello, Karlee. My name is Destin. What can you tell me about those jars?"

"Well," Karlee sniffed, "I thought Scott, he's my fiancé. I thought he was sending them to me. He's interning in Egypt right now."

"What is he interning for?" Destin's gentle voice surprised Dorothy.

"It's a construction company, but they work with a lot of Egyptian digs. They wanted to train him to be a project manager for some excavations in the future, so they sent him there so he could get some training during a dig they're doing now."

"And you thought he was sending you the jars?"

Karlee nodded. "Yes, sir. We don't get to talk very much, but I told him all the shows I was planning to go to right before he left. I thought he was being sweet. Whenever I got back to my hotel room after a show, I would find some of these jars in my room. I thought he had sent them as a surprise, but –" Karlee swallowed hard and blew her nose again. Dorothy set the cup of tea beside her and patted her shoulder.

"When did you receive this pendant, Karlee? Was it before or after the jars began to appear?" Now the man's voice had turned more serious.

"I-I think it was before. I'm-I'm not sure. I'm sorry." Karlee swallowed again. Her bottom lip trembled, threatening to release another torrent of tears.

Destin held a hand up. "It's all right. You have been incredibly helpful, Karlee. Thank you. May I speak to Ms. Fennec now?"

Karlee nodded and handed the tablet back to Dorothy. The woman gestured toward the tissues and tea, and Karlee blew her nose loudly before pulling her knees back up to her chest.

"Send Aaron's message to me. I think I know how to end this, but it'll be some time before I can acquire the artifact that will neutralize the effects of this one and get an agent to you," said Destin matter-of-factly.

Dorothy's brows furrowed. "You plan to use an artifact? But I thought –"

Destin held up his hand to her as he had done to Karlee. "I will have our agent explain things to you when he arrives. Until then, I think it best to remain where you are. Keep the artifact safe. We will be in touch."

The screen went black. Dorothy let out a long sigh. Had Karlee not been present, she might have slouched into the stack of pillows against the headboard. Instead, she placed the tablet back inside her suitcase and grabbed one of the fliers from the hotel that sat on the desk.

"Room services sounds lovely, don't you think?" she asked. Karlee had grabbed the Egyptian jar. Her fingers delicately traced the lines that created a fur pattern, and her eyes stared back into the eyes of the creature.

"You said these jars were meant to hold the organs of the dead," she whispered. "Have I killed them? Are they all dead?"

Dorothy set the flier back on the desk. Her knees cracked painfully as she walked the length of the room and knelt in front of the girl. "I don't believe that for a moment. Do you know why?"

Karlee shook her head but refused to look at Dorothy. "Because Destin is sending another agent to reverse the effects of this artifact. He wouldn't be doing that if he thought the cats were gone for good. And secondly" – Dorothy placed a hand on Karlee's wrist. The girl looked up, her eyes lost and distant – "I know you could never do such a thing. You are too kind, Karlee. Too kind and wonderful for such things to even cross your mind. Now, help me stand up because Lord have mercy, I never should have gotten down here in the first place, and let's order some supper. I see they have a chocolate soufflé."

Karlee finally smiled. She leaned forward and helped Dorothy to her feet, then walked across the room for the hotel flier, the bounce in her step returning.

THIRTEEN

KARLEE STAYED WITH DOROTHY UNTIL SHE began to nod off in the recliner. Dorothy watched as she seemed to finally relax into sleep. She and Frank had never been blessed with children, but her motherly instincts had never left her. She shook Karlee awake and escorted her back to her own room. Karlee stopped in the doorway, staring at the Egyptian jars.

"Can you take them?" she asked. "I just – I can't look at them."

Carefully, they gathered the strange little Egyptian jars and placed them on Dorothy's dresser. Even then, Karlee seemed nervous to leave Dorothy. She bade the woman a tentative bonne nuit before shutting herself in her room. Dorothy heard her lock the door behind her before shuffling away to her bed.

With no cat to show, Dorothy wondered what she

would do the next day. Something was still amiss, but she couldn't place it. The face of Jeff Martin flashed before her. It had been all too easy for Dorothy to convince him to continue with the show. Any normal person would have canceled things long ago, wouldn't they have? But Jeff hadn't argued about continuing, and he and Sharon still had some sort of bad blood between them. It was the sort of thing that shouldn't be overlooked, Dorothy thought to herself.

She opened the door to her room and quickened her pace to the suitcase. The wind had picked up in the last few hours, and it beat hard against the window. Her entire body ached from the change in the weather. All her years in jiu-jitsu had taken their toll on her body. At least that's what she told herself, despite everyone else's remarks about her age.

She grabbed the tablet again and entered the Fox's Den. There were several other buttons she had not yet explored. She clicked on one, and a map with six little dots appeared. They were in clusters of two, and Dorothy realized they were the GPS trackers and audio recorders she and the girls had planted.

Two of the dots were unmoving, but four of them were clustered in a single room and pacing back and forth. Dorothy zoomed into the map until she could see the outlines of the individual hotel rooms. The two dots labeled K.A. were still and sat on the nightstand next to Karen Augusta's bed. Down the hall, Sharon Rhors and Jeff Martin both convened in Jeff's room.

Dorothy touched one of the little dots, and a window popped up with a soundwave file. Dorothy fumbled with the volume button on the tablet, then listened carefully.

"…continuing to put people in danger," said Sharon's voice.

"No one has been hurt, Sharon. Stop being over dramatic," came Jeff's voice more quietly over Sharon's audio recorder.

"No one has been hurt? Jeff, we've had over a dozen cats disappear!"

"They're cats, Sharon. We can breed more," Jeff sneered.

There was a moment of silence, then Sharon seethed back at Jeff, "That is exactly why your cattery is under investigation. Our cats are not money makers!"

"My cattery is under investigation because you decided to stick your nose where it doesn't belong!" Jeff cried. "I sold you one of my finest Siberians, and then you decide to turn around and fix the damn thing!"

"Her uterus was infected, Jeff! And you let it get that way!"

Dorothy watched the dots come closer together, then the ones labeled J.M. backed away.

"That is not true. Bella was fine when she left me. You fixed her so you could change her to the altered category. You knew she could win if she was fixed. You wanted to rub it in my face that you took her to a supreme when I couldn't," said Jeff.

There was another pause and Sharon's dot moved closer to the door. "So that's what this is about? Are you waiting for whatever this is to take Bella? Are you controlling this thing, Jeff, so you can steal her back?"

Jeff's voice was barely audible through Sharon's audio recorder. "Get out."

Sharon's dots hurried into the hallway and toward the elevator. Dorothy fumbled to close the audio window. Sharon had started to cry. She pushed one of Jeff's dots and the window for his audio popped up. She listened carefully but couldn't hear anything except the rustle of papers and a TV playing in the background.

It was nearly midnight. The show would start again in nine hours. Dorothy closed the audio file window, took her nightly medicines, and promptly went to bed.

As she lay in the darkness, she moved her foot, waiting for it to touch the warm body of a feline curled at the end of the bed. But it never came. Her heart beat a little harder, and Dorothy lifted her head. The black cat jar faced her from the dresser. Its green eyes seemed to bore into her. She lay back down, her thoughts racing.

If the artifact could indeed make someone forget a cat, then there was nothing stopping Jeff Martin from using it to steal his cat, and countless others back from their unsuspecting owners. Except he didn't have the artifact. Dorothy did. As far as she knew, Jeff didn't even know what the artifact was. Unless…

Dorothy sat straight up. Jeff might not have been following Dorothy after all. He could have been following Karlee. He didn't know that Karlee no longer had the artifact. Dorothy swung her feet over the side of her bed. She breathed deeply and turned on the light. A winter storm was brewing over the city of Paris, and there was a storm brewing inside her own mind. She walked to the bathroom and poured herself a cup of water from one of the water bottles on the counter. She gazed at her reflection in the dark mirror. She couldn't see the wrinkles that outlined her face, or the bags that hung beneath her eyes. She looked younger and determined.

Dorothy set the cup down beside the sink. Karlee had locked her door. Dorothy had heard it herself. She walked back to the bed, stopping only to turn the little black cat jar so that it no longer stared at her. She buried herself in the giant comforter and mountain of pillows and fell asleep.

It felt as though Dorothy had barely closed her eyes when she heard the hotel alarm beeping in her ear, and she hit the snooze button for the first time in her life. She rolled back onto her pillow and looked out the hotel window across the room. A thin layer of snow had blanketed the city overnight. It reminded her of the cozy nights she had spent huddled under the down comforter with Frank in the early morning hours of winter. They would stay in bed as long as their stomachs would allow. Then Frank would carefully slide out of bed and retuck the blankets around his wife. He would shuffle to the kitchen and put a kettle on the stove. Dorothy would follow suit soon after, sometimes with the blankets still wrapped around her. She sighed and lifted the blankets over her head. That's when she saw the black cat jar facing her again.

She blinked and sat up. She clearly remembered turning the little statue away from her last night. Or perhaps she hadn't. Now wide awake, Dorothy heaved herself out of bed. A cold had settled in the room, and despite Dorothy cranking up the heat, she still shivered. Her knees and hands were particularly stiff and achy. She rubbed her hands together as she hobbled to the bathroom.

As of yet, Dorothy still had no plan. Not officially anyway. She showered and dressed and still had an hour before the show started again. She turned on the television but realized she couldn't understand any of the news anchors, so she shut it off again. Her breakfast arrived on a little cart beneath a silver cloche. A perfect soufflé. Dorothy flipped through the pictures on her phone as she ate. Apparently, her cat – Solomon, was it – had enjoyed a soufflé as well while at the café with her. She smiled and shook her head. She'd never imagined herself owning a cat, let alone one that went to the café with her and enjoyed a soufflé.

She finished off her meal and started packing. She could hear several of the cat show attendees leaving their rooms and clogging the hallways as they headed to the front desk to check out. By the time the last of her blouses were packed, the halls were quiet again. She pulled her suitcase through the door and realized Karlee had not come to visit her yet that morning. She headed up the hall and turned the corner.

The door to Karlee's room was slightly ajar.

"Karlee?" Dorothy called out. Silence.

The hairs on the back of Dorothy's neck stood on end. She pulled the tiny Smith & Wesson from her purse.

The hallway was now deserted, though Dorothy wouldn't have cared if anyone saw her. Her heart beat wildly in her chest. She pushed every fear she had from her mind and crept closer to Karlee's room.

She leaned against the wall just outside the door. She could hear mumbling and someone frantically moving things around in the room – like they were searching for something.

Dorothy reached a hand into her pocket and squeezed the amulet. She slowed her breathing and readjusted the gun in her hand. She nudged the door open with her foot and turned sharply into the door frame. Her eyes widened, and she nearly dropped the gun.

Karlee stared at the wall before her, her mouth slack and her expression blank. Karen Augusta looked up from the drawer she had completely ripped out of the dresser and stopped whatever strange chant she had been murmuring.

"Ms. Fennec," the woman said sweetly. "Please, come in."

Dorothy took a tentative step into the room, her gun

still aimed at Karen. She sidestepped to Karlee and saw the girl was entirely catatonic.

"Oh, there's no need for such things here," said Karen. She lifted her hand and the door to the room slammed shut. Dorothy moved in front of Karlee. Before she could lift her gun to aim again, Karen gave another sweep of her hand, and the gun sailed across the room.

"What have you done to her?" Dorothy demanded. She ran her hand over Karlee's face and tried to shake her awake.

"She is the key to bringing back my grandson," Karen said calmly as she ripped another drawer from the dresser. "It took some time, but I discovered her little necklace is connected to the Gatekeepers of the Underworld. Did you know the Egyptian Book of the Dead is such a fascinating read?"

"Let her go, Karen. She has nothing to do with this, and that amulet isn't what you think it is," Dorothy pleaded. Karen continued to search Karlee's room.

"Isn't it, Ms. Fennec? And what would you know of such things?" She swept her hand behind her without looking, and Dorothy felt herself slam against the wall. She tried to move, but she was frozen. "I only need to make a deal with Thenemi and give Bast enough cats for her army, and they will return my grandson. But what would a simple *Américain* know of such things?"

Karen turned away from the dresser and dug into her pocket. She produced a piece of charcoal and knelt to the floor, drawing symbols Dorothy recognized as Egyptian hieroglyphs. She drew a circle around Karlee and began chanting again.

Dorothy glanced at her gun, which was only a few feet from her now. But she was still trapped against the wall. She struggled against whatever invisible bonds held her and watched in horror as Karlee lifted into the air, her toes just scraping the carpet.

"Karlee?" Dorothy called to her. The girl did not answer.

Karen continued drawing hieroglyphs on the carpet and speaking in what Dorothy assumed was an ancient Egyptian dialect. When she had completed her symbols, they flashed a bright, golden color and Karlee's eyes turned black.

Dorothy fell to the floor, her body wracked with pain. Karen approached her, no longer whispering the strange incantations. "Where is the amulet?" she asked. Dorothy looked between Karlee and Karen, her mind racing as quickly as her heartbeat.

"What have you done to her?" Dorothy screamed. She tried to reach for her gun but felt a force grip tightly around her throat.

"She has been prepared as the vessel for Thenemi. Now, give me the amulet. She will be released when I have finished. Do not think I won't end her and find another. I know the pain of losing an innocent, and I will force that pain on you if you do not cooperate."

Dorothy felt tears coming on. She reached into her pocket and produced the amulet. Karen's eyes flashed with a maddened pleasure. She tore the necklace from Dorothy, her smile becoming more maniacal by the moment. She placed the amulet around Karlee's neck, and the same golden light flashed from the talisman.

Karen stepped out of her charcoal circle and began chanting once more. Very slowly, Dorothy crawled across the floor behind Karen for her gun. As her hands wrapped around the cold metal, Karlee's body stiffened. The amulet opened, and the tiny sistrum beads floated out, turning into a golden dust that hung in midair.

Dorothy held her breath and watched as the dust entered Karlee's mouth. Her body relaxed a bit, but her head cocked awkwardly as if listening to Karen's words.

Karen stopped speaking and Dorothy watched as Karlee's black eyes seemed to study Karen as she spoke.

"Thenemi," Karen said. She took a step forward.

"Guardian of the Underworld, he who comest of Bast
_"

Karen took a single step across the threshold of the circle, and Karlee's hand clenched around Karen's throat.

"*Aleawdat aljaysha, alrraqiq.*" Karlee's mouth moved, but it was not her voice. The palms of her hands began to glow with Arabic script.

"Let her go!" Dorothy demanded. She stood, gun in hand, but aimed at the floor. This was not Karlee, but it was still Karlee's body.

"*Aleawdat aljaysh allliha' wa. Im tat alnnihayat,*" the entity repeated.

"My grandson," Karen whimpered, still clutched in Karlee's grasp. Black eyes turned from Dorothy and back to Karen.

Dorothy lunged, pulling at the back of Karen's blouse. Whatever had possessed Karlee was thrown off guard just as much as Karen, who screamed and toppled out of the charcoal circle. The amulet dangled around Karlee's neck and Dorothy snatched it with her other hand, breaking the chain.

"You want this?" Dorothy asked and she held out the amulet in front of her. Karlee stood straight again, her head tilted and cocked as the entity listened. It stretched out the girl's hand, and Dorothy pulled the amulet back at the last moment. "Let the girl go."

The next thing Dorothy knew, she was lying flat on her back, the edges of her vision still blurry. The side of her face burned with pain. She sat up, looking for her gun again. At her feet, Karen had smeared the charcoal circle as she stood and fled from the room. A ghostly outline of armor was forming over Karlee's body, which had just stepped outside the circle.

Dorothy scrambled to her feet. Seconds later, she heard a loud thud as Karlee's body hit the floor. Where the girl had once stood was now a black-eyed, jackal-headed figure in full Egyptian armor.

The two stared at each other, then the creature lunged, a gleaming spear in hand. Instinct kicked in for Dorothy; she moved in close to the creature and grabbed its human-like arms. She twisted, staying in close and out of range of the spear. She never dreamed her jiu-jitsu would have prepared her for this. But the creature was far too strong. Normally, she would twist her opponent's arms behind their back, and then force them to the ground. She couldn't get the thing to budge. It pulled its arm from her grasp and sent her flying.

This time, her landing was much softer.

"Urgh!" someone cried from beneath her. She rolled to her side, and whomever she had landed on leapt to their feet. They held out a hand to her, and Dorothy swore she was looking into Frank's eyes.

FOURTEEN

IT WASN'T FRANK, BUT THE SHOCK WAS enough to stop Dorothy in her tracks. The man seemed unfazed by the sight of the strange creature in the middle of the Parisian hotel room. His hair was peppered with gray, and his eyes were narrowed from years spent under the sun. He carried a bag slung over one shoulder. Dorothy pulled her gaze away from his eyes and saw a small silver fox embroidered on the bag strap across his shoulder.

"Get the girl," she said, throwing herself into the room again. The creature turned its spear on her once more. Dorothy dodged it, knowing every bone and muscle in her body was going to loathe her by mid-afternoon. This time, she didn't stop to try any sort of infighting. She ran headlong into the jackal-headed figure and pushed it spread eagle onto the bed behind it.

Dorothy heard a grunt from behind her. She balled up her fist and punched the creature as hard as she could in the throat.

"Fennec!" the man shouted from the doorway.

She scrambled off the creature and bolted for the door. As she reached the hallway, she saw the amulet still open on the floor. She lunged for it and gave a roundhouse kick to the back of the jackal-man's knees before running into the hall again.

"This way," she said. The man followed, carrying Karlee in his arms. Dorothy fumbled for her key card as she heard the creature let out a strange sort of cry. Someone in the hall behind them screamed.

"The elevator's this way," said the man.

"No. It's after the jars. They're in here," she said. She opened the door and ushered the man inside, locking it behind him and moving as many items as she could in front of the door.

She turned and saw the man had laid Karlee on the bed and had begun rummaging in the bag. He pulled out several ancient scrolls, an Egyptian aegis, and what looked like a mummified giant scarab.

Dorothy rushed to the Karlee. Her skin was a sickly gray, and her breathing shallow. She hoped the creature didn't have some kind of sixth sense to locate the jars. They needed time to figure out a plan.

"This is my fault. I never should have let her get so involved," Dorothy whispered.

"Did it say anything?" the man asked.

"What?" Dorothy asked.

"The guardian. What did it say?"

"Uh…" Dorothy's heart pounded. She heard more screams from the hallway, this time much closer to her room. "Something about *alnnihayat*, I think," she said. The man turned back to the bag and began rummaging again. "What was that thing?"

"It's one of the forty-two judges of the afterlife. Thenemi, of the Goddess Bast. There's a legend that Bast had an army of cats. Thenemi, a guardian of the underworld, kept them in the state between life and death until the time Bast called them for a sort of – well, we don't know if it's to save the world or destroy every last human on the planet."

Dorothy jumped. Something pounded hard against the hotel door. "How do we stop it?" she whispered.

The man quietly pulled out a scroll and unraveled it. "Let's try this."

"Try?" Dorothy seethed. The pounding stopped. Dorothy and the man looked at the door and saw a shadow beneath the doorframe move away. They both breathed a sigh of relief and turned back to the scroll.

"What do you mean try? You don't know what to do? Who are you anyway?" Dorothy still whispered.

"Agent Red, at your service, Lady Fennec." The man held out a hand with a wry smile. When Dorothy only stared, he dropped his hand and continued, "The interpretations of Egyptian hieroglyphs aren't exact. We have a few options, and one of them should work."

"Let's hope we aren't killed in the process," Dorothy snipped before glancing at Karlee. "What do we do?"

Dorothy's pocket vibrated, and her phone rang loudly. She fumbled with the volume buttons, and instead, answered the call.

"Hello? Dorothy?" came Mary Pat's voice from the other end.

The pounding started again, and this time Dorothy thought she saw bits of wood fly from around the frame.

"Dorothy, can you hear me? You sound like you're at one of those Blue Man concerts?"

Dorothy abandoned the phone on the bed, turning instead to the man holding the scroll for guidance.

"Let it in, hold up the amulet and – you do have the amulet."

Dorothy pulled the necklace from her pocket again and the man nodded. His calm demeanor was comforting, even with a guardian of the underworld beating down her door – quite literally.

"Hold up the amulet and then repeat after me." The man's eyes locked with Dorothy's. She set her jaw, stood a little straighter, and headed for the door.

As she reached for the deadbolt, a spear sliced through the door, missing her shoulder by less than an inch. She shrieked. The guardian pulled the spear back and rammed it through the door again. Dorothy held up the amulet, and the creature paused. It gave her only a second to unlock the door. She twisted the handle and backed away quickly.

The guardian hesitated in the doorway when it saw the dozens of canopic jars.

"Dorothy, are you in Vegas? What is going on?"

The creature let out its strange cry when it heard Mary Pat and took a step forward.

"Hail, Thenemi," the man said behind Dorothy.

"Hail, Thenemi," Dorothy repeated, holding the amulet aloft.

"Who comest forth from Bast."

"Wh-Who comest forth from Bast." Dorothy swallowed hard, her fingers trembling as she watched the creature stop and cock its head the same way it had done when possessing Karlee.

"I have not acted the part of the spy or eavesdropper," the man continued.

"I have not acted the part of the spy – really?"

The creature let out its strange cry again and started to advance on Dorothy once more. As it passed the canopic jars, they turned to the same golden dust that had escaped the amulet.

"Right, didn't think of that," said the man. He began rummaging through his bag again.

The guardian reached back a hand and tried to stab Dorothy. She ducked and attempted to sweep the creature's legs out from under it. But it was like hitting a tree trunk. The jackal creature did not move. Instead, it turned its gaze toward the man rummaging in the bag. It pushed past Dorothy, stepping on her foot in the process.

"Look out!" she cried to him. She leapt on the creature's back, her arms tight around its neck.

"*Aleawdat aljaysha, alrraqiq,*" it said as it stopped before the man. Nearly all the canopic jars had turned to golden dust and trailed behind the guardian. The creature readjusted the spear in its hand and ran the man through.

"No!" Dorothy screamed. She looked at the black cat jar on her dresser. She swore it was staring at her again. She jumped from the creature's back and snatched the jar from where it sat. The guardian's head snapped up, but she did not stop. She raced to the window and wrapped her already throbbing hand in the curtain. She punched through the window and thrust the jar through the jagged glass.

The creature had started to move toward her, its spear raised in threat despite its seemingly calm demeanor. It halted once more when Dorothy dangled the jar through the broken window.

"Revive the girl, and you can have your army," she said. "For whatever purpose it serves, it must be worth at least her life."

The guardian tilted its head again. Dorothy had no idea why it kept doing so – it was more disturbing than its solid black eyes. It turned toward Karlee, who still lay motionless on the bed. The creature's palms glowed with hieroglyphs as Karlee's had, and Dorothy saw color return to the girl's cheeks. It turned its gaze back to Dorothy and held out its hand.

"Aleawdat aljaysha, alrraqiq." The creature's voice was steadier this time.

Dorothy hesitated, then pulled her arm back through the glass. Her arm dripped with blood, but she ignored it. She took a tentative step forward, keeping one eye on the spear.

An elaborate Egyptian aegis appeared around the creature's neck. The golden dust of the jars fell and returned to the cat canopic jars once more before hitting the carpet. The guardian cried out, but the man who had been run through held on tightly. Dorothy lifted the amulet before the guardian. She heard the man begin to speak in a strange language, and the jar in her hand started shaking. She set it at her feet just as it transformed back into Solomon. She felt dizzy and unsteady as her memories returned. Solomon jumped onto the dresser beside her and shoved his head under her arm, helping her keep the amulet aloft.

Dozens of cats milled around the guardian's feet, hissing and growling. The man continued chanting, and Dorothy saw the guardian begin to fade into a ghostly façade. There was a flash of golden light, and the amulet in Dorothy's hand snapped shut. The guardian was gone. The man swayed, and the aegis dropped from his hands. Dorothy rushed forward and led him to the bed.

"You – were amazing," he whispered before abruptly passing out.

FIFTEEN

THE NEXT FEW HOURS WERE A BLUR. DOROTHY immediately contacted Destin, who sent in a team of paramedics and various men and women in gray suits. Karlee came to after the medics gave her an injection. Much to Destin's displeasure, Dorothy allowed her gaggle of girlfriends to enter the room to see her. They squealed and cried, and Destin finally kicked them out when Karlee was carted off to the hospital.

Karen Augusta had been found in the lobby restroom and had immediately been arrested. Her grandson's stuffed animal cat had been placed in a plastic evidence bag.

Dorothy wasn't sure what to think about Karen. If she had had the opportunity to bring Frank back, would she have done the same? Dorothy wrapped her arms around herself as Karen was pushed into the back of a police vehicle. The woman watched as her grandson's stuffed cat was shut into a metal briefcase with the other evidence bags and hauled away.

The cats were wrangled and secured. Their "distribution," as someone called it, was being handled by a very tall, burly man in a navy-blue suit and wool trench coat. He carefully placed them in carriers, scratching each on the chin and speaking softly to them with a gentle smile.

"Charlotte!" Jenna cried when she saw her Siberian. The burly man handed the cat to her, and Jenna squeezed the cat so hard, Dorothy was sure the cat's eyes were about to pop out of its head.

The man who had helped defeat the guardian seemed to have dodged any major internal damage. When Dorothy heard the news, she let out a sigh of relief she had not realized she was holding in. The man glanced at her and smirked.

"Worried about me?" he said.

Dorothy blushed. "Well, of course! I'm sure it would greatly affect my acceptance into The Foxes if an agent had died on my first mission."

He chuckled and reached out a hand to her again. "I'm Red."

Dorothy shook his hand and felt the hair on the back of her neck stand on end.

"You mentioned that," she said and felt her cheeks flush.

"You have good instincts, Ms. Fennec. Like your father, I hear."

She released Red's hand before he could feel hers begin to shake. "You knew my father?"

Red nodded. "Only briefly. I-I haven't been with the agency very long myself. Probably why they sent me. I don't think anyone realized this mission would be so –"

"Dangerous?" Dorothy finished. She shuddered and pushed away the image of the jackal-headed creature as it had stabbed Red.

"You have natural instincts for this job, you know," Red continued. "Holding that jar out the window and holding out the amulet to keep him away."

"I don't know why it worked." Dorothy shook her head.

"It was his prison," said Red. "Thenemi is one of the forty-two judges of the underworld. He was created by Bast to assist Anubis with transitioning the souls of the underworld. But what Anubis didn't know was Bast had another plan for Thenemi. He was charged with protecting the souls she sent to him using her magic sistrum. These souls were to be kept until a time when she would call on them for some unknown purpose. That amulet was the link between Thenemi and the transportation of the souls to his care. But it also meant his entrapment. Each time Karlee used the amulet, it created a connection between her and Thenemi like his connection to Bast. But, I think he discovered a way to turn the tables. He could speak through Karlee and control her until the amulet was opened and Thenemi could take his true form. He had only to return the souls of Bast's army to the underworld, and he could be free to roam the earth. To what end, I do not know. And this is all speculation anyway."

Red shifted on the bed, wincing and suppressing a gasp of pain. He smiled again when he saw Dorothy's look of concern.

"Don't look so nervous, Ms. Fennec," he said. "We'll be on a plane back to the States in no time. I'm sure Artie's already got his little metal box warming up."

"I highly doubt you'll be traveling anytime soon in your current condition, Mr. Red," said Dorothy.

"Then I suppose I will have to look you up when I return."

Dorothy's phone rang in her pocket. She was thankful for an excuse to turn away from Red's gray eyes.

"It's my sister again," she said.

"Ah, the Vegas one?" Red asked.

Dorothy chuckled. "I'll think of something to tell her." She swiped the screen to accept Mary Pat's call, then immediately held the phone at arm's length.

"Dorothy! Are you at a strip club? What's with all the sirens? You are in Vegas, aren't you? Why didn't you invite me? Is that Magic Mike I hear?"

Solomon seemed more clingy than usual. And not only on the plane ride home. Dorothy slept the entire flight with the cat curled up on her neck and chest. He even demanded to be held and carried around her apartment and the antique shop for the next three days. Dorothy had no idea what had happened to him during his time as a canopic jar, but she was glad his personality hadn't changed. He was her last connection to Frank, and she still couldn't believe she had forgotten the cat entirely. The thought still made her sick to her stomach.

A week later, Solomon had resumed his post on the bed in the window, except this time, the cushion had been replaced with the one from Miss Kitty.

The little bell above the door rang, and Dorothy looked up to see Aaron enter with a large, sealed tube.

He knocked the snow from his boots and shook out his braids.

"I will never understand why you people love this awful sky dandruff so much," he grumbled.

Dorothy laughed and came around the counter to take his coat. "There's hot water in the coffee pot for tea," she said. "Did Veronica send any documentation with the scroll?"

Aaron handed Dorothy the large tube and an envelope. "Yes, ma'am, but she said you may not like the answer."

Dorothy frowned and opened the envelope as Aaron headed toward the coffee machine. She unfolded the paper, and her frown deepened.

"Aaron, will you watch the shop for a moment?" she asked. The young man gave her a thumbs up as he sipped from his coffee mug.

Dorothy headed toward the upper apartment door. It was still painted a sickly avocado green. Solomon meowed and bounded up the stairs ahead of her. She ignored him and headed straight for the secret passage. Solomon seemed to have anticipated her actions. He paced before the bookcase, then trotted down the stairs when she pulled the lever to open the secret door.

Dorothy's nose was still buried in the letter from her

friend at the Smithsonian. She had installed battery-operated and motion activated lights along the side of the winding stair and on the ceiling of the long hallway. She looked up only long enough to open the door to what she had come to call her father's vault.

When she reached the tattered parchment beneath the glass case, she finally set the paper aside and opened the large tube. Inside was the scroll that had been stored in the antique shop case. She set it beside the parchment that lay beneath the case and studied them closely.

After several minutes, Solomon bounded toward the door. Dorothy looked up and saw Destin enter, the black cat draped across his shoulders.

"Your welcoming committee has improved since last I was here," he said.

Dorothy walked to him and relieved Destin of the cat.

"What can I do for you, Mr. Hollanday?" she asked.

"You have not responded to my emails or letters," he said. "It is not my nature to stalk my agents, but in this case…"

Dorothy huffed and shook her head before letting the cat down. She walked back to the scrolls, followed closely by Destin.

"I see you have discovered the scrolls of

Aramanthia."

Dorothy continued to stare at the parchments. "I had a friend of mine look at this one," she said as she nodded toward the larger piece she had pulled from the tube. "Veronica has studied linguistics quite extensively. Do you know what she found?" Dorothy finally turned to Destin with an accusing sort of stare. "Nothing. Absolutely nothing. The most she could decipher is that this is only one of many pieces. Its contents are unknown to her, as they contain variations of letters from several languages, and most of them have been lost in time to any sort of translation. My father had been studying this scroll. He even had Aaron researching it for him on occasion."

"What are you implying, Ms. Fennec?" Destin asked.

Dorothy narrowed her eyes at the codename she had come to detest. "You told me my father was ill, though his doctors assured all his family that he had passed from natural causes. His heart was weak, and his kidneys had shut down." Destin licked his lips but remained silent. "This scroll has something to do with his illness."

Destin smoothed his hair flat. "Ms. Fennec, it would be wise for you to leave such matters alone. I came here today to find out if you are accepting my invitation to join The Silver Foxes. If not, I have a truck on standby to remove your father's artifacts immediately."

Dorothy straightened her shoulders. "I have no intention of giving up any of these artifacts until I discover the truth about my father's death. And if you will not help me, then I'll continue on my own."

Destin sighed and gave a single nod. "Very well. In that case…" He pulled a large envelope from the inside of his coat and handed it to Dorothy. "This is your next assignment. But don't worry, you won't be doing any field work for a bit. You're on research duty for Red this time."

"How is –?"

Destin answered her question by handing Dorothy another sealed envelope. She opened it and found a letter from Red. She smiled, then remembered Destin was still watching her.

"Tread these waters carefully. This organization is not a dating club." Destin fixed his homburg on his head. He leaned down to scratch Solomon before heading for the door. "Welcome to the Silver Foxes, Ms. Fennec."

Dorothy looked up from Red's letter. "Mr. Hollanday?" she called. Destin stopped in the doorway. "My name is Dorothy Claes."

ABOUT THE AUTHOR

C.P. Morgan, or Cassandra Penelope Morgan, was born in a small town in Ohio. She comes from a family of both writers and English majors from both sides of her family.

The idea for the Silver Fox Mysteries was inspired by stories she heard growing up about her grandmothers. She also writes YA Fantasy under the name Cassandra Morgan.

Cassandra is a frequent guest at conventions and writing conferences in the Midwest area. She is a writing coach, a foster for orphaned kittens, and participates with The International Cat Association.

Connect with Cassandra!

WWW.AUTHORCASSANDRAMORGAN.COM
WWW.AUTHORCPMORGAN.COM
CONTACT@AUTHORCASSANDRAMORGAN.COM

FACEBOOK: **/author.cassandra.morgan**
TWITTER: **@AuthorCasMorgan**
INSTAGRAM: **@Morgan_Cassandra**

MORE FROM C.P. MORGAN

Book Two of the Silver Fox Mysteries
Prowl of the Yule Cat
Coming Fall 2018

C.P. MORGAN WRITES YA FANTASY AS
CASSANDRA MORGAN

Coming Soon
Spring 2019
Book Two of the Kingdoms of Chartile series
Magic

DOROTHY CLAES

AND THE

PROWL OF THE YULE CAT

THE WOMAN CHUCKLED. "ARE YOU HERE visiting family? Most travelers don't come until its warmer."

A gust of wind blew hard against the window behind Dorothy as if on cue. "Business, actually. I own an antique shop in the States."

The woman nodded and fiddled with something in her pocket anxiously. "I suppose many of the families here will be getting rid of some of their belongings. They're relocating now that the warehouse is closed. And what with the…" She trailed off, squeezing whatever had been in her pocket tight in her hand.

"I'm sure there's an explanation," Dorothy said,

setting a consoling hand on the dark-haired woman's arm.

She nodded and swallowed. "There is. And it's not the trolls, no matter what anyone says."

Dorothy tilted her head. "You don't believe what everyone's saying?"

The dark-haired woman scoffed. "That the Yule lads are using their mother's giant cat to steal little girls to be their brides? No. It's ridiculous."

"What do you think it is?"

The woman squeezed the object in her hand even tighter. "Something far more human." She was silent for several moments, and Dorothy saw her pocket the object again. "Well, as I said, I wanted to apologize for upsetting Solomon. I won't keep you. *Góða nótt.*"

She turned on her heel almost as quickly as Ada had done and disappeared down the tiny staircase.

Dorothy closed her door for what she hoped was the last time that night, and deposited Solomon on the bed.

MAGIC

THE FIRST THING CHARLIE NOTICED WAS THE smell. It was the smell of lush grass, sweet, and of course, his one allergy. He lay there, his eyes still shut, waiting for his body to erupt in a red-hot itching rash. But it never came. He dared to open his eyes, wondering where his glasses had fallen to, and found himself in a large clearing in the middle of a dense forest.

The second thing he noticed was that he was stark naked. How he hadn't noticed before, he had no idea. Charlie quickly looked around the clearing. There was no one around. Covering himself to the best of his ability, he darted for a mass of bushes straight ahead. He found a leaf on the ground behind the bushes the size of a dinner plate. He wiped the dirt off, and used this to cover his front.

Panic was beginning to set in. Was this some sick joke Malcolm's friends were playing on him? He wondered if there were cameras somewhere. Maybe behind him at this very moment. Charlie found another dinner plate-sized leaf on the ground, and quickly covered his rear end. He had to get out of here, and fast. But, where *was* he?

Charlie looked at the trees and bushes around him. Some looked vaguely familiar, but most everything else was entirely foreign. Not a single maple tree anywhere, and Fulton County was notorious for its maple trees.

"Okay, don't panic," Charlie said to himself. He reached up to push his glasses up his nose, and realized they weren't there. How could he see without his glasses? He was legally blind without them. His heart was pounding so hard in his chest, he was ready for it to burst out and begin flopping around on the ground in front of him.

Charlie felt a warm, humid air across the back of his neck. The hair stood up, and he turned around very slowly. What he saw was not what he expected to see. Charlie stared into the bright golden eyes of a black panther. It grinned back at him, showing a level of intelligence that terrified Charlie even more than being so close to a wild animal.

"If you were to run," the panther whispered to him, "It would be all the more fun for me."

It took only a second for the realization that an animal had just spoke to subside before Charlie bolted back out into the clearing. The panther threw back its head and gave a kind of laughing roar before taking off after Charlie.

9 781732 139824